True Savage 6

Lock Down Publications and Ca$h Presents
True Savage 6
A Novel by *Chris Green*

Lock Down Publications
P.O. Box 870494
Mesquite, Tx 75187

Visit our website @
www.lockdownpublications.com

Copyright 2019 by True Savage 6

First Edition March 2019
Printed in the United States of America

Lock Down Publications
Like our page on Facebook: Lock Down Publications @
www.facebook.com/lockdownpublications.ldp
Cover design and layout by: **Dynasty Cover Me**
Book interior design by: **Shawn Walker**
Edited by: **Jill Alicea**

Stay Connected with Us!

Text **LOCKDOWN** to 22828 to stay up-to-date with new releases, sneak peaks, contests and more…
Thank you.

Submission Guideline.

Submit the first three chapters of your completed manuscript to ldpsubmissions@gmail.com, subject line: Your book's title. The manuscript must be in a .doc file and sent as an attachment. Document should be in Times New Roman, double spaced and in size 12 font. Also, provide your synopsis and full contact information. If sending multiple submissions, they must each be in a separate email.

Have a story but no way to send it electronically? You can still submit to LDP/Ca$h Presents. Send in the first three chapters, written or typed, of your completed manuscript to:

LDP: Submissions Dept
Po Box 870494
Mesquite, Tx 75187

DO NOT send original manuscript. Must be a duplicate.

Provide your synopsis and a cover letter containing your full contact information.

Thanks for considering LDP and Ca$h Presents.

Dedication

This book is dedicated to Allah, the most high. Without your guidance and firm religion I would be another lost soul on this earth. To my brother Barry Mathis, I apologize that I never got to make good with you on our situation. I love you Bro, R.I.P. and know that you'll always live in my heart. To my daughter, the prudent and intelligent Cerenity Green, I love you, Baby. My mother, always and forever, you are the sun that brightens my day. I love you more than anyone on this planet and those are BIG Facts! And of course I have to thank the ones who didn't think I could make this awesome ass series.

Acknowledgments

I want to thank all my fans even though I'm on lockdown and I can't talk to all like I use to. I miss you all and love you all very much. To all my queens, Shanika, Dianna, Doris, Melita, Michelle, Tanisi, Candice, Khloe, Kayla, Valerie, Samantha, Kristina, Niecey, Miyanna, and Reshonda, I love you all and pray that you are growing daily, spiritually and mentally. A big shout out to my mentor/idol Jay-Z, Shawn Carter, for making the Black album. I sit back on my bed every day, soaking up your inspirational words to be a better young Black man. It has encouraged me to go head first for what I truly want. The same for my second mentor, T.I , Clifford Harris. Kosa quote: "You will either be greedy, or eat away your future or you will starve and sacrifice for your success. "To the Kings of my family, Uncle Green, D-lo, Tim, Wild, Devin, we will always win! Last but not least, I would like to thank my boss Ca$h and the entire LDP family. They can lock me in the hole for five more years and we still gone drop heat. To my sister, Destiny Skai, these hating ass police just want to stop our greatness, lol! We still gotta handle our business. Shawn Walker, our COO, so stern, lol! You still help mold the best writers ever. With that I love you all and know that I'm still pushing. I hope you all enjoy!

Chris Green

Prologue

Destined for Death

"Well, I met her a few years back before I left for New Jersey to further my career in law enforcement. I was assigned back to a case in Georgia and upon arrival, she contacted me and says my assistance was needed."

"How did she get in contact with you and what exactly did she need your assistance with?" he questioned, with his arms folded.

"She found me through recent associates of the Magic City Gentlemen's Club. When she finally reached me I was asked to be a part of the family structured drug ring that was in operation," Courtney exposed while slanting her eyes towards Reeses's.

That one hundred percent of walking out of the building instantly crashed down into the bottom of a hope and prayer box as she listened to who she thought was Camilla spill her secrets. She cursed herself for letting an outsider slide through the cracks of family business. Not including that she happened to be DEA.

"And what exactly did Ms. Rivers ask of you when you accepted this position," The DA asked ready to throw Reeses under the bus.

Her mouth was about to produce the magic words until her eyes locked with a familiar face that sat in the back row of the courtroom.

Her mind began to stutter as he stared her down with a death-like expression. The only difference of his appearance was the long scar that ran from the bottom of his right cheek to the middle of his throat.

"Ms. Myers? Can you answer the question, please?" The judge ordered, breaking her attention.

Looking at all the faces that waited to hear her response, the DA quickly switched questions.

"Have you ever witnesses Ms. Rivers trafficking narcotics?"

Swallowing her spit in fear, she answered in a troubled tone, "No."

"Excuse me? Do you hear what you're saying, Ms. Myers? Have you ever witnessed the suspect personally dealing with crack cocaine?" His voice boomed with intimidation.

"No!" she repeated while watching the man walk smoothly out of the courtroom.

Her chest heaved in a frightful manner realizing how close he'd gotten to her without being noticed.

"Sir, we demand an immediate release and dismissal of all charges on my client. Your state and I will clarify again more clear, your courtroom, has yet to show anything that's sticking to her. It's quite obvious their witness here feels the same way," Harvey stated with a pathetic face.

"What the hell is wrong with your witness? She's going to screw up this entire case," he mumbled to Agent Smith through slanted lips.

"You can't just expect her to talk with you being over aggressive. She just went through a tragic moment of her life and I think you're scaring her."

"I'm gonna have to agree with the defendants side on this matter for now. I won't be dismissing it for probable reasons that Ms. Myers is under too much pressure from the incident to testify. But I will grant a hundred thousand dollar bond for the lack of evidence the state has offered. I'm setting a two week date to get this together. If it's not, I'm dismissing all charges and throwing out the case," the judge ordered, banging his gavel.

If looks could kill Reeses's grey eyes would have ripped Courtney's heart severely from her body as the guards led her back to the holding cell.

For the last few days she laid in her bunk with numerous of emotions running a mile long. The dull white walls and metal sliding doors only made things even worse. The day she was arrested was like death date in her mind until Harvey showed up for an attorney visit. After confirming that he was a family representative and Mariah was highly pissed. He guaranteed that she would be out within a week. The moment for that had finally arrived and Reeses was anxious to release all of her anger. Her mind was set on spilling the blood of all her snakes in the grass. Starting with Courtney!

Chapter 1

Two hours later

Feeling the burn from the ammonia invading his nostrils, police chief Myers finally opened his eyes with a massive pain thumping through his head. His palms were sweating profusely. Both wrists and ankles were bound and both his legs felt as if they were broken. As the blurriness cleared from his pupils, he focused in on the man standing in front of him.

"Where in the fuck am I?" He cringed in pain while looking around the filthy garage.

"You're exactly where you're supposed to be, Captain. It's been awhile but I can't say that it's a pleasant reason why I'm here." The man stated truthfully with an evil glare.

"I don't think you are aware of what you're doing, jerk-off! I don't know who the fuck you are but I'll give you thirty seconds to release me from these restraints and we can act as if this never happened."

The hard steel barrel that crashed across his nose broke it instantly, sending him into a panic.

"Aghhh, motherfucka!"

"Your time is up, Myers. You touched the wrong family. Instead of you doing your job, you stuck your nose into business that was far too deep to breath. Does Jimmie Rivers run through your head when you think about that remark?" Ghost asked picking up a small red container of gasoline.

The fear in his eyes gave away the truth as he stuttered over his speech.

"I don't know what the hell you're talking about, Jimmie Rivers has been dead for ten years!"

"Because of you!"

"Bullshit! His own brother took him out. I sat across the street and watched it with my own two eyes," he screamed as Ghost emptied the entire container of gas over his head and clothes.

"That information is unnecessary. He's next on the list," Ghost said in a heartless tone before lighting a small piece of a dirty cloth.

"Wait! Wait! I can" was all he could spill before his body turned into a blazing torch.

"Aggrhh! Goddd! Nooo! Nooo!" he yelled in horror as the flesh of his face slowly peeled from the flames that covered him.

The smell of burned skin flowed through the air while he shook uncontrollably to free himself. Sparking a menthol Newport, he inhaled two pulls and watched as Myers tortured movements ceased. Walking out of the garage Ghost made his way down the driveway of the abandoned home. After checking out his surroundings, he jumped inside the two door Ram truck and pulled off slowly.

Cobb County Jail

Walking out of the front doors of the detention center Reeses laid eyes on the man who made it all possible. Arthur Harvey, the family lawyer waited patiently on the sidewalk with a briefcase dangling in his hands.

"Ms. Rivers, it's great to see that you were released in a timely fashion. I've arranged for a speedy trial next week to get these false accusations dismissed. You shouldn't have anything to worry about," he spoke with confidence before a black Tahoe truck came to a halt in front of them.

"Thank you," she replied while watching Laylah roll down the passenger window.

"No problem. The Grey family always seems to be my first and main concern. The pleasure is all mine."

Nodding in appreciation, she began to head towards the vehicle.

"Ms. Rivers?"

Turning around she waited for him to speak.

"Please try and stay clear of all trouble if you don't mind," he warned with a cautious expression.

"I'll try," she uttered before opening the back door of the truck.

Seeing the wild dread head Jamaican Knox sitting in the driver's seat, the hairs on the back of her neck stood up. His eyes drifted towards her as she slid into the backseat.

"Harvey wanted to have you out earlier but couldn't pull the strings until you walked in the courtroom. Are you okay?" Laylah asked looking back.

"How did you all know I was locked up? I never made any calls the entire week."

"Knox followed you. It was the reason she warned you not to leave, Reeses. Keeping things low-key with this family is like putting a baboon inside of a cardboard box and telling it to be quiet. It's no telling who's looking to finish us off the same way they done the rest of our kin."

"It wasn't my intention to run into a jail cell Laylah. I just wanted to straighten things out with my brother and his team. I didn't want to leave without them knowing what was going on," Reeses sighed letting out a deep breath.

"Try telling that to her."

Sitting back in the seat she got the answer that was expected. Mariah wouldn't care for an excuse because the warning was given up front. Her experience with running the operation was a success which means her words shouldn't have been taken lightly.

It seemed as if it took forever for Knox to reach the new house in Kennesaw, Ga. A home that was recently purchased with Mariah's outstanding face-card and healthy savings account. The spacious six bedroom home sat on ten acres of land. The humongous black steel gate that surrounded it guaranteed to hold for security purposes and if it couldn't the nine armed guards who posted behind it were sure to sweep the problem under the rug.

Pulling down the narrow driveway, Knox parked the truck directly in front of Mariah who stood by her new 2017 Range Rover. Stepping out of the car, Reeses locked eyes with Mariah and could feel the anger rising off her skin while she held an IPhone close to her ear. Her Dolce and Gabbana lace fitted dress hugged her luscious curves like glue. The black Gucci pumps that were laced around her feet spelled the word TASTE in four different languages and her silky brown hair was pulled back and pressed into a French roll.

"What gave you the initiative to take my car and leave after I gave you specific instructions," Mariah asked, hanging up the phone on her current conversation.

"Just like I told Laylah, I have my own strings out here in Atlanta and I refuse to leave them untied. You're not the only one who has business to handle, Mariah."

"Business is discreet. What you are doing is moving sloppily and it'll eventually crumble this entire family. It was never in my plans or schedule to make you apart of anything dealing with this operation. My mother is the only reason you're even standing in front of me and my sister. She wants you in the islands immediately. It's for your own safety, Rinesha."

Shaking her head she folded her arms with a firm stare.

"I know that I mean nothing to you and trust that I'm not stressing that at all. I've made my own way since I was sixteen and never received an ounce of help from anyone. Lots of people use the word family and stab you in the back before you can turn in a full circle. The problem I have on my hands isn't going to stop unless I end it myself. Leaving the situation in the air can cause this shit to fall directly back on us all. Don't you get that? Or do you have your arrogant head shoved so far up your ass that you just don't care?" Reeses asked with a hint of hostility in her voice.

"You need to choose your words carefully, little cousin. I spent my entire teenage years handling millions and getting rid of problems that threatened to harm this family. I'm the fucking Renaissance woman in this game when you speak of handling issues and I'm only a year older than you. You say that you have a problem, let my man fix it and we can continue about our way with clean hands."

"I'm afraid it's not going to work that way, Mariah. I'm very thankful for the family standing in my corner and when this is done I will take my position with you all and stand on it firmly. This is personal. I'm not asking for permission but I need you to have respect for my wishes and trust in what I'm saying," Reeses voiced with a serious expression.

Taking a breather Mariah lowered her gaze with a sympathetic expression. It was unlike her to accept requests or orders from anyone besides her mother. Respect was something that was only given to loyal associates and family and at that time Reeses was the closest blood within their presence.

Walking over to her they both stood eye to eye without blinking.

"I'm going to give you two weeks. If it's not handled by then I'll bring closure to it all and I will drag you down to the island myself."

"So does this mean I can help her?" Laylah butted in with a slight smirk.

"It means you can assist, it doesn't mean go overboard, Laylah. And just to let you know every action you take will have to be answered for when we get back home," she addressed Reeses before getting into her Range Rover and pulling off.

"No one has ever made Mariah change her mind about anything after she gives our mom her word. What exactly are you trying to do?"

"I'm gonna cause havoc on everyone that crossed boundaries against me. Friend or family!"

Nodding with and evil smile, Laylah turned her head to face Knox.

"Take us to Atlanta."

Chris Green

Chapter 2

It was five minutes after twelve when Shaun pulled his car in front of the small efficiency lodge. Rolling down his window he pressed two buttons on the small speaker box to contact the designated hotel room.

"Who is this?" the voice asked speaking with a shaky tone.

"Buzz me inside the fucking gate!"

There was a slight pause after his words before the mechanical fence began to slide back, allowing him to enter.

Pulling around towards the back, Shaun parked his car and headed up the stairs to the second floor. Walking through the breezeway of the extended stay he reached room two oh eight and knocked three times. There was small movements and sounds that could be heard on the other side before the door opened.

Slick held his gun in hand and cautiously glanced back and forth before stepping to the side.

"Are you sure you're by yourself?" he asked with a paranoid ass expression like the entire top floor wasn't empty.

"Ain't I'm the only fucking person you see?" Shaun replied moving past him swiftly.

Looking around the room his eyes landed on Samantha. From the last time he saw her it looked as if her head gained sixty pounds. Her hair was beginning to thin and she obviously didn't recognize he was in their presence because her attention was on the pure fish scale cocaine that was scattered in small piles on the wooden table.

"I came to holla at you about the rest of my paper for that contract," he said, getting straight to the point.

"What? Nigga, that bitch is still breathing, right? How can I pay for a job that ain't been handled, Shaun?"

"First off, lower your fucking voice, I'm standing right here. Second, word around town is your niece had something to do with my sister being murdered."

"And what does that have to do with me?" Slick questioned with a hint of worry.

"It has a lot to do with you when your family is involved, nigga. This is the beginning of a serious tragedy and it's all about to fall down on your head."

"What the fuck are you talking about?"

"You've been sitting in this room getting so trashed by the dope that you haven't even thought to look at the news. Your blood was on the scene of a dead detective from the Smyrna police department. You and my father have officially made public enemy number one," Shaun replied with a sinister smile.

Captain Myers flashed through his vision after hearing the remark slide into his ears swiftly like a Q-tip.

"Son of a bitch. I guess yo pussy ass daddy sent you to murder me, huh?" Slick asked scooting closer to his handgun just in case things turned sour.

"If I was here to kill you, I would've splattered your shit when you first opened the door, stupid ass nigga. I think the police want you more than my father. Besides, they just found his body burned alive inside an abandoned shed. He can't do you any harm, but I can."

"What the fuck do you want from me, Shaun?"

"First, I want the rest of my money from the contract you thought about running off on. Next, you're going to help me catch this bitch and kill her."

"And if I choose to say fuck you and I refuse, then what?" Slick replied in an arrogant manner.

Shaun smirked with a light chuckle, "Humph, then my sources will make sure you're in a cell and a wheelchair for the rest of your miserable life. All you gotta do is say the word."

Slick's mind began to register the threats that were being delivered to him on a silver platter. It was for sure that Shaun had a slimy motive, but it was unclear on what devilish plot rested in his brain. His instincts told him to pick up the gun and see which one of them had acquired the best aim, but the look that laid in the young killer's eyes told him he wouldn't be successful with his actions.

"I'm listening."

"Good, I'll be through at eight o'clock to scoop you. Try not to get any funny ideas," he warned before walking out.

***

Walking back and forth into the living room of Shakur's home, Stone waited anxiously for Reeses to show up. The trip last week to the Virgin Islands turned extremely sour after he realized the wrong person was being followed. Mistaking another female for Reeses, he fell directly into a trap that nearly cost his life. It was indeed the mercy of Allah that Laylah stepped up and mentioned to her mother that he was a bodyguard for her cousin. Being held captive for two days by a house full of Jamaicans told him that something way out of his league was about to occur.

"Ahk, I really don't trust this bitch pulling up to our house. It's like you trying to chase death, bro," Salim said sitting on the couch in front of him.

"I'm not chasing anything but the truth. Regardless of how you look at it. Justin needs to know what the fuck is going on. There's more to this story that we haven't read yet and I'm tired of it all being in the dark. She owes me an explanation," he stated calmly while rubbing through his beard.

"What more of an explanation do you need, Ahkie? You just almost got yo head severed off a few days ago by a gang full of Zoe Pounds. I think that's clear enough," Shakur added.

Bang was posted against the wall quietly listening to the men speak back to back about the situation. Pointing towards the window at the black Tahoe pulling inside the driveway, they paused their conversation.

"You're going to get us all killed, my nigga. Certain shit is just meant to be left alone, Stone. We got too much on our plate and I'm starting to think this bitch is out to get us," Salim said heading into the bedroom.

Watching him with a curious eye, Stone opened the front door allowing everyone to enter.

"Hold up, who the fuck is he? You can't come in here, my nigga, but you can definitely wait on the front porch," Shakur stated placing a hand on Knox's chest.

"He's with me, these are my people. Relax," Reeses commanded with a hint of aggravation.

"I don't give a fuck if he was with Donald Trump. We don't know this motherfucker!"

Laylah's hand moved to the small of her back pulling a black and chrome Glock 9 that was placed between Shakur's eyes.

"I don't think we had a chance to get acquainted either. My name is Laylah and this is Knox. We're here for my cousin and her only. Any questions?" she asked in a sweet voice with a firm grip on her gun handle.

Stepping between them, Stone raised his hands before things could spiral out of control.

"Can everyone just calm down? Please! We don't have time for this shit!"

"You right, I'm calm," Shakur spat with venom in his voice before walking out of the house.

"Stone, this is my cousin, Laylah."

"Trust me, an introduction is not necessary."

Sensing that he was mad about the incident with her aunt Tiffany in the islands, she decided to skip the small talk.

"Listen things are very hard to explain right now. I'm trying to piece shit together in my head, but there's too much coming at me. I got a bad feeling that something terrible is about to happen if we don't take care of these people right now."

"Reeses, I was under the impression that you knew consequences can arise from our actions. You pushed the button on this problem and now you can't contain it. Now either you know something that I don't or the people who claim to be your long lost family are playing you like a video game on easy mode."

"You wouldn't understand right now. This is bigger than me, you, or Justin. We got one week to clean all of this up or we're all going to be spending the rest of our lives in prison or even worse, dead. I can't make you help me but I can ask you to trust me. I need your assistance with putting this to rest. You're the only people I can trust right now besides them," she said truthfully looking at Stone, Salim, and Bang.

"What exactly are you trying to do, Reeses?"

Taking in Stone's question she pondered before answering.

"I need to get rid of everyone we've dealt with within the past month, friends, clientele, everyone. It's the only way we can guarantee that all of us will be safe. Starting with that snitching ass bitch, Camilla. I'm going to set up a meeting with Chi to grab one last supply before we snatch up Justin and get the fuck out of here."

"Wait! Did you just say Chi?" Laylah asked, cutting her off before she could speak again.

"Yeah, why?"

"Reeses, Chi is a Japanese pedophile. He turned into a Federal informant four years ago after one of his businesses was raided. He's a worker for the DEA."

"How do you know this?"

"Because my mom use to supply him with heroin before he was placed under a witness protection program by the authorities."

Feeling her anger start to rise, Sue's face ran through her thoughts. There wasn't a doubt in her mind that she was probably being set up the entire time. Rubbing a hand throughout her jet black hair, she looked over at Laylah.

"He needs to die first then. We can't just jump out here moving sloppy trying to find out who crossed you when there are four or five different motherfuckers we after," Salim added.

"He's right. We have too much on the line and one slip can cripple us all. We've moved Justin to three different hospitals within the past three days. Sooner or later people are going to start asking questions."

"To be honest it's quite simple. People expect the obvious which is for her to come looking for them one by one. If we all spread around and move quietly... let's just say you can't touch"

"What you can't see," Stone finished off her sentence.

"I guess what's understood doesn't have to be explained. You might actually have a half decent team on your hands after all. Let's just hope they can perform the same," Laylah challenged before heading out the front door.

Chris Green

Chapter 3

Clayton County 7:48 pm

The sun had just began to drop below the horizon as Reeses and Laylah cruised through the Clayton County city limits. The mission on their mind was quite simple. Eliminate all problems before her speedy trial that was in seven days. After the legal situation was cleared up Jason would be transferred to the best medical hospital in the islands and the girls would leave Atlanta in their rearview. The product Tiffany was pushing into the states was coming straight across the water from Cuba, Havana. It was only right to send the girls back into the city to re-stamp what was rightfully hers.

Pulling the all black Navigator into the overcrowded parking lot, Laylah stopped the car and smirked at Reeses.

"Showtime. Knox will you take the front seat, please," she said before opening the driver's door and getting out.

Following her lead Reeses climbed out sporting a two thousand dollar silk Georgette dress. Her hair was hanging freely to the middle of her back and her feet was laced in a pair of black Jimmy Choo heels.

"Remember all you here to do is dump the contents inside of his glass and the rest will work on its own."

"And what if he doesn't accept anything to drink? Then what?" Reeses asked before making it to the entrance doors.

"He's a fucking pedophile. It shouldn't be too hard," she replied before opening the door and walking in.

The energy inside the hookah bar, owned by Chi was live and almost packed to its full capacity. Couples lounged around making out and enjoying the taste of the loud marijuana that could be smelled from outside the building. Remembering Laylah's instructions she scanned the room with her eyes before walking to the bar.

"Wassup, pretty lady? What can me get for you?" The older Japanese woman asked with a sincere smile while wiping down the countertop.

"I'll take a small glass of water for now."

Nodding, she grabbed a bottle of Aquafina and placed it in front of her.

"Do you know by any chance if the owner is here tonight?"

"Who Chi? He's always here. Do you have an appointment?"

"Not really, I'm here to surprise him. He's a very good friend of mine."

Winking her eye she smiled and held up one finger before coming from behind the bar station. Reeses sat quietly watching the woman disappear through an open door frame that led to the back.

Looking around, her eyes landed on two guards who walked through the spacious area observing all movements. Judging from the girls that maneuvered with different men to the back, flavored tobacco and marijuana wasn't the only thing Chi was into selling.

It was about five minutes later when the woman reappeared motioning for Reeses to follow her. Spotting Laylah sitting in the corner she assured with a smirk that everything was okay.

Walking through the rear of the hookah bar the scenery switched from a smooth lounge to a midnight strip joint. Women moved about giving massages and foot rubs while the waiters delivered drinks and fruit to different stations. Stepping through a private section of the area Chi sat on a large red silk rug surrounded by four Asian women.

"Sir, your guest is here," the woman said grabbing his attention.

Raising his head his eyes locked in on Reeses and scanned her body up and down with a sly smile. Standing to his feet he moved towards her with open arms.

"To what do I owe for this surprise visit?" he asked in a low voice.

Embracing him in a firm hug, her lips grazed his ear before speaking.

"Just a drink and conversation."

Mumbling something in his native tongue the half- naked women began to leave. Smoothing out his Dolce & Gabbana shirt he checked the time on his Hublot and led Reeses over to a circular suede couch to take a seat. Grabbing two champagne flutes, he picked up the bottle of Rhum Clement X.O and sat beside her.

"Is there a reason you didn't complete our deal? I was expecting business to be in effect by now," he stated filling the glasses to the rim and placing them on the table.

The ringing of his cell phone interrupted their conversation causing him to answer it quickly. It was all the time that she needed to drop the clear substance into his flute without being noticed. Hoping it dissolved before he ended the call she crossed her legs and waited patiently.

"I'm very sorry, darling, that was an important issue that had to be handled. Where were we?" he asked placing his phone on silent.

"About the business," she replied showing off her smooth, thick legs.

Allowing his eyes to roam down her petite curves and body, he placed a hand on her thigh.

"All you have to do is tell me what you need and you can have it if you truly desire it."

"Is that right?" Reeses questioned, grabbing the champagne.

"In Japan being right means to guarantee. I've always been a man of my word," he bragged before downing his drink.

"Okay, I guess since we have an understanding, I can cut to the chase. Things have been said that shouldn't of been mentioned and the heat is falling down on my team. Someone is talking and if we are going to do business in any kind of way I need to know that I won't crumble from anything coming from your end."

Rubbing the center of his chest, his heart began to pump forcefully sending a sharp pain through his body.

"Excuse me," he paused, coughing loudly thinking it was the expensive liquor they'd just consumed.

"Are you okay?" she asked not truly concerned.

"Yes, please continue."

Before she could speak, another cough erupted violently, causing him to kneel over. His vision began to blur slightly as the pace of his heart thumped at an awkward rhythm. Standing up Reeses took a step back and began to giggle.

"I knew I would have to find Sue before I could come to you, Chi."

"What have you done to me?" he cringed in pain while holding his stomach.

"I'm afraid it's what you've done to yourself. The DEA wasn't mentioned in our agreement, Chi. Neither was me being a young sex slave for you like Sue. I guess we have to aim high for what we truly want, huh?"

"You stupid little bitch," he mumbled, feeling his life fade in and out.

Strutting to the entrance she paused before leaving out.

"My Aunt Tiffany sends her love."

The name was the last thing Chi heard before his heart collapsed, killing him instantly.

Moving swiftly back to the front of the hookah bar, Laylah took her position behind Reeses and left smoothly out of the front door.

"Who's next?" Laylah asked knowing without a doubt that the hit was successful.

"The sickest person I've ever met in my life," Mariah replied before hopping in the car and leaving the scene a complete mystery.

***

It had been almost two weeks since Wild left them behind in Atlanta. Being on the run made every place feel like it was closing in on him. It was hard to keep a low profile without having anyone to move for you. Especially in an unfamiliar state where cops roamed daily. Every news station in Georgia was broadcasting his face for the so-called murder of Courtney Myers and according to the reporters the man hunt wouldn't stop until he was in custody or deceased.

Driving inside the Rent-a-Room complex, he pulled into the back and killed the ignition. It was a fact that Memphis was a little too active and the time limit on sitting still was officially up. After stripping the car for parts to sell for extra cash, he opened the trunk and found a small gray handbag inside. Things seemed to be normal until he unzipped the tote revealing the contents. Picking up a large stack of brown files his nerves grew uneasy after viewing the letters F.B.I.

on the first folder. Opening the documents his eyes fell on a black and white photo of a mysterious man. 'Extremely dangerous' was boldly printed at the bottom of his brief profile and the thick packet of papers that sat behind it was guaranteed details on how and why.

After scanning through half of the files Wild couldn't believe the information he held in his hands. Quickly moving up to his rented room he grabbed the burner cell phone that was purchased a few days prior and dialed Stone's number.

***

Hearing the firm knock on the door, Samantha dropped her crack pipe on the floor thinking that Slick must have had a change of plans. After stuffing the rocks inside of her pocket, she tried to kill the smell before unlocking the door.

"Can I help you?" she asked staring at the unfamiliar face that stood in the breezeway.

"Where is Slick?" Stone asked calmly.

"He's not here, probably won't be back for a few hours. Does he know you were stopping by?"

The pistol that curved around the corner of the doorframe caused her body to stiffen in fear. Bang stood in silence holding the chrome 357 at the center of Samantha's mouth. His eyes told her that he would pull the trigger instantly if he heard the wrong sound or movement. Placing a finger over his lips, he motioned for her to back inside the room allowing Reeses and the crew to slide in directly behind them.

"This is an excellent place to hide when you have a group of killers searching for you," Laylah said sarcastically before taking a seat.

Samantha gazed around the room at the two women and three men nervously before Reeses walked over to her.

"I can't recall who you are, but I'll try to make this very simple, sweetie. I am here for one person, Slick! Now where is he?" she asked with hatred dripping from her tone.

"He's been gone for almost thirty minutes!"

"We can see that. Any idea where we can find him?" Stone asked.

"No, I swear. A man named Shaun came to pick him up and they left in a black car. That's all I know," Samantha answered shaking faster than a stripper.

Shaun definitely wasn't a name that Reeses expected to hear connected to her cunning uncle. Tons of treachery was being spilled on their entire circle which meant nothing was impossible. While she thought silently an important rule of the game clicked in her mind. "Nothing beats the cross except the double cross."

Closing the space between her and Samantha, Reeses began to put her plan in effect.

"I know that you don't have anything to do with Slick and the slimy shit he's put me through. If it was up to me I wouldn't have you in the middle of this at all. But trusting you right now is like putting a brick of cocaine around a powder junkie. It's hard."

"Please don't kill me!" Samantha mumbled thinking that her brain was four seconds from being blown onto the wall behind her. "I'll do whatever you need me to. Just tell me."

Stone's cell began to ring, turning everyone's attention towards him. Observing the unfamiliar digits on the screen he answered and placed the phone to his ear.

'Who is this?"

"Asalamu laikum, we got a problem."

"Wild? Walaikum as salam! Where are you and what's going on?" Stone asked grateful that his little brother was okay.

"Where is Reeses?"

Passing the phone to her, she glanced at Laylah before speaking. "How are you?"

"Not too good. I'm moving state to state and trying to stay as low-key as possible."

"That kinda sounds good to me, Wild. It probably wouldn't be smart of you to stay in one spot."

"That's not what I'm talking about. I went through the bitch's trunk and found something. I think y'all need to be the ones getting the fuck out of Atlanta and I mean now," he said with a concern and urgency in his tone.

"What did you find?"

"Something that'll put your entire family and close friends away for the next three generations," he replied seriously.

Not trying to build a case against herself on the phone, Reeses quickly changed the subject.

"I need you to switch lines and call back. I don't want to take any chances with a private listener tuning in on us."

"Reeses! Keep your eyes on Justin," he mentioned before hanging up.

Knowing that he was worried about her brother's condition, she made a mental note to herself. *Handle the differences in the streets and skate out of state with a clean face.*

Staring at Samantha with her mind full of cruel intentions, Reeses held the phone out toward her.

"If you don't want to die for his mistakes, call and tell him to get here. Now!"

Nodding her head, Samantha grabbed the phone as she trembling in fear. After dialing his number into the keypad she pressed the call button and placed it on speakerphone.

Chris Green

Chapter 4

Riding around with Shaun was getting weirder by the second, as he pushed the whip through the streets of Smyrna. He searched for any sign of Reeses and her crew. Slick was jamming a plastic straw into his powder sack every three minutes. Driving in the car with Shaun felt as if he was in a sinking ship with the devil himself.

"So you mean to tell me this is your niece and you don't know where this bitch is playing at? Don't seem like you looking too hard to me," Shaun uttered before taking a chug of drug polluted orange juice.

"I told you before we left, smart guy, this girl ain't on no ordinary shit. You gotta let her come to us without being aware of who she's coming to. Nobody's heard any word from her out of Smyrna in almost two months. Looking for her over here is a waste of time."

"No! Touching my family was a waste of fucking time. Maybe you should've warned Reeses about how I get down before she made this stupid ass mistake!"

Feeling his phone go off in his pocket, Slick pulled it out, watching Samantha's name flash across the screen.

"What is it?" Slick answered slightly agitated.

"Umm, Sheldon, what time do you think you'll be back?" she asked with a small crackle in her voice.

"What! Bitch I ain't been gone more than two hours, I told you I was pulling out to handle something."

Shaun couldn't help but to cut his eyes over wondering if someone was actually on the other end of the phone. His killer instincts smelt fuck shit a mile away and if it was necessary Slick would die sitting in the passenger seat.

"It's starting to feel kind of funny sitting in this room alone. Come back and fuck me or something. I'm lonely."

"Stop shoving all that candy up your nose and fall the fuck back. I'll be there when I get there."

"Good! Because if you're not I'm going to kill her and hunt you down myself," Reeses stated before taking the phone off speaker.

Jerking the phone away from his ear he quickly turned his head towards Shaun before the set of police sirens sounded off behind them.

"Shit!" Shaun mumbled, tucking his gun in between the seat and center console. "Don't say nothing."

"I'm not about to wait around and see if you know how to talk to these people," he replied reaching for the door handle.

Before he could take action on fleeing four black suited officers exited the vehicle aiming different semi-automatic rifles.

"Get your hands up and step out of the fucking car!" One man shouted while pointing the gun at the driver's window. Opening the doors both men were forced to the ground with handcuffs placed around their wrists.

"Damn, Fuck man! Can anyone tell us what the fuck is going on," Shaun shouted with hostility.

"Shut the fuck up!" the officer commanded slamming the handle of the M-16 on the middle of Shaun's face, knocking him unconscious.

After watching Shaun become a quick victim, Slick decided to remain silent until further notice at a bond hearing. His mind was processing how he would throw the entire case on him until a pistol crashed across the back of his head. His body tried to fight the blow until another one followed it.

***

Slowly opening his eyes, the throbbing and dizziness on Slick's brain slowly began to wear off. He was laying on the floor still in handcuffs when his vision started to become transparent. Shaun laid directly next to him staring into space with a bullet hole in the center of his head.

"Good evening Mr. Rivers. I'm so glad you're finally able to join us," a woman's voice spoke, catching his attention.

Sitting up, Slick looked around the spacious mansion nervously before his eyes settled on the Spanish queen who sat in front of him.

"Don't worry about your friend, after he awoke from his short slumber he began to act belligerent. But now that he is at peace. I figured that me and you could have a conversation. Please take a seat," she motioned at the metal fold out chair in front of her.

Sensing that his life was about to be taken at any second, Slick slowly stood to his feet and took a seat. The same four men who he'd assumed to be the authorities stood in different corners praying for him to make the wrong decision.

"Do you know or have any idea who I am?" she asked in a calm manner.

"No. But judging from the knot on my head and your fake ass police squad I can bet you're about to tell me," Slick spat holding the side of his face.

There was no chance in hell on bucking and even if he did think of trying it he was bound to die before getting the opportunity to stand out of the chair.

"You and me both seem to have a similar problem on our hands. Over the years I've learned to have more discipline but as time passed patience and self-composure have finally taken their toll. This young girl that you're running around for, I need you to bring her to me," Eva stated with a firm stare.

The small chuckles from Slick caused one of the men to deliver a solid punch to the center of his jaw. Jumping up on his feet to react the barrel of an AK-47 was pressed to his cranium.

'Sit your ass down, before I make you take your last piss and shit lil' man!"

Easing back down into the chair he smirked at Eva with rage burning in his eyes. It was clear that she was in charge and dying was definitely not on the schedule before leaving out of his hotel room.

"Who the fuck are you?"

"Who am I? Mhmm! Let me see, I'm just a scorned woman in need of a few favors. You've always been a complete fuck up and that's okay. I'll make things simple for you. I'm willing to let you keep your life and walk out of here a rich man if you can complete one mission," she stated, lighting a long menthol cigarette.

33

"And what would that be, Ms. Deblanco?" he replied sarcastically, in reference to the well-known drug queen from the movie Cocaine Cowboys.

"Bring Rinesha to me. When you find her there will be two more girls tagging along. I want them all here, now!"

"Fucking with this little bitch right now is like suicide. She has too many motherfuckers watching her every move. It's impossible to get the drop on her without somebody dying."

"Well, I guess that means you'll die trying."

"Why do you want her? What is she worth to you?"

"Everything and more."

Slick couldn't help but wonder about the strange woman and her comments about Reeses. Although he hated to admit it, chasing Reeses' ass for this long and trying to get the drop on her next move had become a real headache. Her mental prowess was no longer average, as it had been during their first encounter. After everything he'd recently lost within the past month, the next move was to get as far away as possible from the problem. In this case that problem was Reeses.

"I'll do it."

Inhaling on the strong nicotine Eva crossed her legs forcing a small giggle. Years of pain and torment of losing her three boys was a critical rock to climb over. Now was the time for payback. Every resource, every connection was being pushed into making one person suffer. A person she hated dearly. Ghost.

"Wise choice, Mr. Rivers, I'll be in contact and my men will drop you off where they picked you up. And for the record if I found you once I can find you again," Eva threatened with a devilish grin.

As the guards forced him to stand up, Slick turned around and laid eyes on a young beautiful blonde headed woman who was posted on the living room's doorframe. The holster on her waist concealed a black, stainless Sig Sauer handgun and her arrogant facial expression told him that she wouldn't hesitate to use it.

Dumping the ashes of her cigarette, Eva watched as Agent Smith moved toward her. "I know that things didn't go as planned but I can assure you all will be taken care of very soon."

"There's a reason you were paid to handle this mission, Smith. You had all the tools to use so that our hands could've stayed clean in this matter and you still failed. How am I supposed to feel about that?" Eva asked standing to meet his gaze.

"We know that you're gonna feel the way you want to, Eva. But I also have five other agents who are in cahoots with this case. If I make the wrong move everything is going to fall."

"I gave you one point three million dollars because of something you agreed to. Now if it seems impossible to handle, place a rope around your neck and hang yourself from the nearest bridge. You're excused, Smith," she replied putting the cigarette butt out against his bulletproof vest.

Nodding his head he quickly made his way out of the home.

Turning her attention towards the blonde headed teen Eva smiled.

"Patience, Frost, in due time my princess. You'll have your revenge and a little more."

"I've heard that nice song ever since I was seven years old," she replied looking down at Shaun's body on the floor.

"And that song has finally come to a dead end," she smiled before lighting another cigarette.

***

Downing another shot of Tequila, Reeses meditated on her complex problems at hand. The loss of family was growing by the month and deceit within her circle was spreading by the second. Thoughts of her grandmother and father's strong love was starting to weigh heavy on her heart. It was also tough to lose so many of your greatest supporters and still stand firm throughout it.

As she closed her eyes feeling the late night breeze Stone stepped out on the back porch and took a seat beside her.

"I guess now is not a good time for you to talk?" he asked admiring her beauty.

"There's never really any space for talking but that doesn't mean I won't listen."

Nodding, he removed his kufi and took a deep breath. "When I was sitting in a prison cell a few years ago with a life sentence I awoke everyday with the same question on my mind. I asked Allah, would I ever receive a chance to be the person I truly knew I could be. A chance to prove that I actually had a purpose for this place we call home. After eight long years my prayers and answers were finally given in full."

Sitting up straight she began to tune into his words.

"I told myself that I would be placed where I was truly needed and I landed here."

"You're here because you want to be, Stone. There's nothing magical or religious about it."

"I'm here because I need to be, Reeses. I see that the serious situations happening with this family is about to drag you under. Your path was never meant to crumble, your heart wasn't placed inside you to be broken. All the things that you are going through, they still carry a purpose."

"And I'm guessing you're going to tell me what purpose that is?"

"Telling is something I've never been good at. But showing you is a choice that you will have to accept from me in order to see."

Grabbing her hand he kissed her fingers delicately before standing to his feet.

"The only way you can win this situation is to let it be. You're very prudent for your age and wisdom is key that's not given to everyone. Don't let your key lock you out of the door from what you have yet to learn," he said before walking back inside Shakur's home.

Talking was something that usually fell on deaf ears when it came to her business but the truth was hard to deny regardless of who voiced an opinion. Things wouldn't be changed until a graveyard swallowed all her grimy ass enemies one by one.

Chapter 5

It was nine thirty in the morning when Stone made the call for everyone to meet at Shakur's home. They sat in silence pondering the next move after receiving the mysterious threat from Reeses's phone.

"There has to be some type of way to trace a name down on that number," Stone said in think mode.

"I told you, it's impossible. The phone company has a private communication service line. All they produce is throw away phones. When you purchase one the information on your account can easily be placed under an alias," Laylah stated.

Reeses sat there looking amused as she viewed. Shaun's mutilated body on her screen. She felt a great sense of satisfaction that a major problem had been resolved without having to involve her crew. But the text message that was delivered with the attachment spooked her even more.

Scrolling down, she read it again slowly.

"This is a day that I have waited patiently for. A chance to actually confront the people who ruined my life. It felt so good to place a bullet between your little problem's eyes that I almost came twice before pulling the trigger. Now that I've finally released a little steam I can choose my words carefully for you all. I'm going to kill you one by one. Personal issues are supposed to be handled in a personal manner so I will be brief. Surrender to us and I will make sure that all of your deaths are as painless as possible. After all what is family for? Tell my lovely stepmother I said hello. Frost."

Her mind was puzzled about who she was dealing with. Lately bullshit was sliding from different avenues and it was guaranteed for a distinctive purpose. If Shaun was dead and Slick was ducking and dodging for his life, it would be impossible to see the secret enemy who planned her demise.

"I'm not sure, but I think I've heard of the name Frost before. We need to go and talk to Mariah," Laylah suggested.

Moving towards Reeses, Stone pulled her to the side.

"Something isn't right about this issue. Now I'm not positive about what's going on, but I think you need to keep all thoughts and movements to yourself until we unmask this situation."

"Agreed, send everyone over to Mariah's and go inform Justin about what's going on. No one is to make any moves until we find out who the fuck we are dealing with."

Staring into her grey pupils he opened his mouth to speak but his words just wouldn't spill.

"What?" she asked sensing that something else was on his mind.

"Nothing," he mouthed, quickly snapping back into his mode. "I just want to let you know I'm here."

"You never had a choice, remember?"

Nodding, he smiled at her arrogance and grabbed his gun as the crew made their way out of Shakur's home.

***

Northside Hospital

Walking into the entrance of the medical building Reeses and Stone made their way to the elevators and headed up to the fourth floor. After making it upstairs he paused before moving through the double doors.

"I'm gonna use the restroom and meet you at Justin's."

"Okay."

Stepping inside the men's room he washed his hands and began to splash the water across his face, looking in the mirror. Stone took a breath and thought about the twisted situation that he was stuck in. His feelings for his brother's sister were growing by the day. The honor to protect her was valuable and it was a mission that he would complete by any means. His bond with Justin was always tight as ever and in order to keep that connection he would eventually have to express the truth to them both.

Grabbing a paper napkin he dried his hands and headed back out to the lobby. His mind was so distracted while coming out the restroom that he bumped into Shakur sending him to the floor.

As he looked up in Stone's eyes his heart started to beat at a quick rate.

"Shakur? What the fuck are you doing here?"

"Man, I just came to holla at Justin for a second and was on my way back to the spot," he stuttered while standing up.

Gently bobbing his head he looked into Shakur's face before walking off.

"Asalamu-laikum."

"Walaikum- as Salam."

Stone was always able to smell a liar from a distance. No one knew the whereabouts of Justin but him and Reeses, which made it highly strange for Shakur to be inside the hospital.

"Why don't you come around to the room with me and we can all leave together?" Stone stopped and asked as he stood in front of the elevator.

"No thanks, Ahkie. I just can't stand seeing the brother in that position. We can link back up after you leave from here. Insha-allah," he uttered before the doors opened.

Strolling quickly, he made it to Justin's room where Reeses sat with him in deep conversation.

Looking over at Stone, Justin couldn't help but smile. No matter whether he was having a good or bad day his brother's demeanor would never change. Humble, stern and always there for a Muslim no matter what.

"It's good to see that you're still overly aggressive, Ahk. As- Salamu- laikum."

"Walikum as Salam, bro. How long did Shakur sit around here with you?"

"Shakur? That nigga ain't came to see me. You know him anyway, probably in the mix of some business. Money keeps his mind elsewhere," Justin confirmed with a small chuckle. "Is something wrong, Bro?"

Playing the scene back in his head he was careful to keep an eye out for any false movement coming from the brother.

"Nah, everything is Alhamdullah. How are you holding up?" he asked, making his way closer to the bed.

"Truthfully I just want to be around my friends and family. A lot of shit is really fucking with me but I'm so grateful to still be here with y'all."

"First of all stop talking crazy like you going somewhere. We're always going to support and stand by your side no matter what. Shit has been crazy out there but we're trying hard to end things as quietly as possible," Reeses stated with a serious expression.

"Things will work out in your favor in the end. You're a winner, Muffin. It's in our bloodline to prosper."

Soaking in his motivational words she began to think of her accomplishments within the past five months. Her losses had been reimbursed times ten, but the gross still showed that things were not greener on the other side. Grabbing his hand, Reeses looked into his face with sincere eyes.

"Do you think we should just say fuck it all? Just take the money we got, invest in a few businesses and move out the States? We can all just disappear and never come back."

"I want nothing but the best for you, Rinesha. And yes, I agree with leaving, but situations that we have in Atlanta are problems that will last a lifetime and you just don't need that. End it all here. When we leave it won't be such a thing as looking back."

Stone sat back and listened to the two of them speak while he ruminated on certain affairs. The ability to use his knowledge effectively was the reason he had yet to fall. It was common sense to see that Reeses was fighting a losing war.

It was impossible to beat something that you couldn't see. Instead of leading Reeses away from the chaos, Justin was pushing her towards it. Regardless of the next man's actions Stone's mind was focused on one priority. To ensure that Reeses made it out. Even if it meant giving his own life.

***

Pulling back in front of the house, Salim parked his car behind Shakur's and jumped out quickly. After arriving at Mariah's crib he realized he had forgotten his lifeline and made a U-turn.

Stepping inside the front door he paused after hearing Shakur yell as if he was in deep conversation. Trying to keep a low profile, he moved swiftly to the corner wall and spotted him standing in the kitchen.

"No, I'm not around them. We haven't discussed the money yet. I don't know this woman so how can you guarantee that I'll get my paper if I snatch this bitch? Okay I'll do it. Just call back and let me know," he mumbled before hanging up the call.

As Salim maneuvered into Shakur's vision, nervousness spread across his face.

"Who were you talking to?"

"Where in the fuck did you just come from? You scared the shit out of me, bro," he replied placing a hand on his chest.

"I said who were you on the phone with?" Salim asked a little more aggressively.

"I was just chopping it up with my man Ahkie. What the fuck is your problem?"

"So what bitch your moms wanna snatch up?"

Biting on his bottom lip, he pulled his .45mm from his waist with ease.

"Don't even think about reaching for that shit!" he spat with venom in his voice.

"Let me guess, the business man decided to take matters into his own hands and cross out his brothers. Are the Feds gonna kick in the door now?" Salim asked with a face of pity.

"Nah, no Feds, but you gonna need the police and a few ambulances if you thinking of stopping this paper flow."

"I knew you could never change, Shakur. It's in your heart to be a slime ball and you've proved it once again."

"A half a million dollars doesn't make me slime, it makes me smart. After Slick offered me the deal I couldn't take it back, Salim. My life is on the line and I'll choose me over her any day. Just help me and we can walk away together, Ahk. We don't know this bitch," he offered with his finger caressing the trigger.

"My duties are to Allah. I stand firmly by my brothers because that is the Iman and Islam inside of me. I can't allow you to harm that girl. Period!"

Shaking his head in disappointment, Shakur pulled the trigger sending a bullet into Salim's abdomen.

Boc!

Releasing a gasp, he grabbed his stomach before crumbling to one knee. Looking up he eyed Shakur as the blood began to pour through his hand.

"Allah is the witness of all your deeds, bro, I pray that he curse you to experience the worst death possible," Salim said while breathing harshly.

"Allah knows my heart little brother. All I wanted was a better life and I can't help if you guys want nothing," he spoke before delivering another slug to his chest.

Boc!

Moving quickly he wiped his prints from the pistol with a kitchen rag and placed it in Salim's palm. His mind was speeding in a panic causing him to drop his cell phone on the carpet before rushing out of the door.

***

Six Flags Drive

"Just like I told you, if she's not trying to comply with what I'm asking, I'll get rid of her," Agent Smith said before hanging up the line.

Stepping out of his black Crown Victoria, he trailed up the driveway towards the witness protection safe home. After Knocking and ringing the doorbell once, he waited patiently until Agent Mays answered with an uneasy expression.

"Greg? How did you know I was here? This location is supposed to be classified information," she asked while shifting to the side so he could enter.

"I am a F.B.I. agent, Courtney, it's my job to know things that people are trying to hide," he replied closing the door and engaging the locks.

Giving him a displeased look she walked towards the small living room.

"Please save all attitudes for a later day. I have too much climbing up my ass with this case and too many superiors treading for information just for a promotion."

From the looks of her hair and empty bottle of Chardonnay on the floor, he could tell her mind wasn't settled.

"You're putting too much pressure on yourself, Courtney. Why don't you just step down from the case and take a few months off," he suggested hoping she would agree.

"Excuse me? These idiots tried to fucking kill me, Greg! I truly didn't care about the River's family because they are not who I am after. Chance Grey was my only concern and Rinesha slid right in the middle of it all," she complained with an angry tone.

"And that's understandable, you have to decide which is more important. Your safety, life, and sanity or proving a bunch of assholes that they're criminals."

Agent Smith was trying his best to convince her to get out of the picture. Things were starting to get past serious and if she didn't take heed things were going to end tragically with a slug being placed between her eyes.

Taking a deep breath she leaned back on the couch.

"I've spent my entire career waiting to see if their asses were actually dead. Maybe you're right, it's probably just time to take a break and do a little office work," she lied trying to change the subject.

Taking a seat next to her, Smith cleared his throat before speaking. "Sometimes we spend our energy searching for answers that'll never be found, Courtney. The most devious and clever schemes bloom from the ones who can remain unseen. Take my advice and steer clear from this situation. Please," Smith stated with a stern face.

"Relax, I'll think about it and that doesn't mean I'm saying no, before you began your next lecture," she uttered with closed eyes.

His instincts told him to spray her brains over the couch and let Eva instruct him on the rest of his duties, but his weak and lustful heart wouldn't let him pull his weapon.

"Make your decisions wisely, Courtney. I don't want to see you get hurt."

As he moved towards the door, Courtney eyed him suspiciously until his presence was gone. Picking up her phone she placed a call.

"Myers?"

"Good evening, sir. Requesting to go active," she replied into the receiver.

Chapter 6

Staring up at the hundred thousand dollar crystal chandelier Mariah sipped on a glass of Chateau La'fleur Petrus while she listened to Stone speak. Her temper was boiling through the roof and her ears had finally heard enough.

"If it wouldn't be too much to ask, I would like you to please shut up for one minute so I can speak!"

Rubbing his beard, he quietly took a seat and glared with a heated expression as she stood to her feet.

"First off, thank you Rineshia for bringing these total strangers to our home. I see you've tricked my little sister in to coming along with you on this ridiculous ass trail of failure. Now is there anyone in this room that can tell me why aren't we on our way out of the states," she asked, looking around the dining room full of people.

"Like I said."

"That was a rhetorical question," she blasted cutting Reeses off. "It doesn't have to be answered because the answer is sitting right in front of me. I'm sorry to be the ruthless truth teller on this silly ass situation. But my family placed me in charge of this job to do one thing. Bring her home."

"Mariah, we weren't just fooling around out there. We've been moving the best we can for the past two days and extra shit continues to surface. We aren't just chasing a few enemies. We're at war with our own family," Laylah admitted with a straight face.

"What in the hell are you talking about?"

"I remembered you mentioned the name Frost to me before or am I just imagining things?"

Mariah could feel the goosebumps crawling over her skin after hearing the name roll off Laylah's lips.

"Excuse me for a minute," she mouthed standing to her feet and walking out of the dining area.

"Can you please tell me what's going on? What do you mean we're at war with family?' Reeses asked with a nervous expression.

"I'm kind of lost and need to know the same thing," Stone said with a slight attitude.

"Frost is supposedly a seed of my father. I'm not quite clear on the full story just yet and unfortunately Ms. Bossy Mariah didn't inform me of this wonderful news until a month ago."

"How in the fuck are we supposed to handle any of this if we have blood fighting blood? Things are getting a little too complicated. Maybe moving around with each other might not be so good after all," Reeses suggested looking over at Laylah.

"There's nothing we can do about that, Rinesha. I told you when we first met this family has secrets and issues that will never end. It's more of a tradition. The sad thing about it is, we don't even know who birthed this problem to existence."

"So, basically there's a psychopathic woman running around claiming to be your sister and no one even knows if she's telling the truth?" Stone added.

"All of us are missing a few screws but she's definitely telling the truth. Our father was just a donor for a freak who has yet to reveal herself."

Walking back into the dining room, Mariah massaged her temple before speaking. "It looks like we might be here a little longer than I expected."

***

Super 8 Hotel

"Fuck this pussy, daddy," Rose moaned in excitement, as Slick entered her from behind.

Using a small bottle of KY jelly he spread the liquid across her butt while he stroked her slowly. The vanilla shampoo that lingered on her body enticed him even more as she looked back into his eyes. Her womanhood began to flow with the length of his dick, soaking him with every motion.

Feeling the urge to nut he pulled out of her rubbing his rod up and down her warm and juicy pussy lips.

"Please put it back in," she whined spreading her cheeks apart so he could see how pink her kitty was.

Ignoring her he bent down and placed his tongue between her folds and began to lick away her juices as if he was on a mission.

"Oh my god, Slick!" she yelped as her eyes started to roll in satisfaction.

Rubbing her round and voluptuous behind he twirled her clit with his fingers causing her body to tingle with delight and pleasure.

Standing back up to his feet she wasted no time turning around until her face met with his manhood.

"It's so big," she teased groping him with two hands.

Twirling her tongue around the tip of his dick, Rose took him into her mouth and smacked as if it was a giant lollipop. Watching him lean his head back she held her breath and began to deep throat his piece slowly.

"Fuck!" he grunted, grabbing the back of her head.

Holding her mouth wide he started to slowly pump back and forth watching her gag from his girth.

"Lay on your back," he ordered, rubbing through her hair.

Twirling her fingers around her nipples, she eased back on the bed and spread her legs. Climbing on top he slid back inside of her tight walls while she placed kisses on his chest and neck.

The loud knocking on the room door caused him to freeze and look at Rose.

"Who the fuck is that?" she asked stopping his motion.

Jumping out of the bed, Slick slid on his pants and grabbed her burner off the dresser. Moving past the corner wall, he tip-toed swiftly and looked through the peep-hole.

After seeing who was on the other side, he relaxed and opened the door.

"Nigga, why in the fuck are you knocking like the fucking police?" he mouthed, looking Shakur up and down.

"We got a problem!"

"What do you mean a problem?"

"I killed one of my brothers. He walked in on me and you talking earlier and eavesdropped on the conversation," Shakur replied shaking his head.

"What the fuck does that have to do with me or Reeses?" Slick asked, slightly aggravated.

"Because I killed him in my fucking house. They're gonna know it was me, my nigga. I didn't have a choice. If I didn't get rid of him he was gonna fumble the whole plan."

"And it also means they're gonna be on alert for your dumb ass. Your only job was to snatch the bitch and bring her to me."

Rose peeped her head slightly around the corner after hearing Reeses name. Spotting Shakur's slimy ass, she knew that the two was obviously planning something that she wasn't about to be a part of.

"If you feel like it's so easy, my nigga, you wouldn't need me for shit. The bitch is being treated like she's Queen Elizabeth and I'll probably catch a bullet in the back of my fucking head before I can grab her."

Grabbing Shakur by the collar of his shirt, Slick pushed him against the door and pressed the barrel of his gun to his right eye.

"If you felt that you couldn't handle this simple ass mission you should've continued to be a do boy for that bitch. You accepted, now I want progression. Find a way to make it happen before you are swimming in the fucking creek before your twenty-fifth birthday," he threatened before releasing his shirt.

Nodding in compliance Shakur straightened out his shirt. He knew his gangsta was just tested and he wanted to reply by placing a few hot ones into Slick's chest. Instead of letting his anger decide, he vowed to catch him on a later day after all their business was settled.

"I'll get it done," he stated before leaving out the door.

Adjusting the locks back Slick turned around to find Rose fully dressed with her things in hand.

"Where the fuck you think you going?" he spat with a menacing glare.

"It's starting to get dark and I need to make my way to work before I'm late again," she replied just as her phone started to vibrate loudly.

"Who is that? Your boss?" Slick asked with a skeptical look on his face.

"Umm! No, it's just a friend. I'll call you when I get off."

As Rose reached for the doorknob, Slick grabbed her weave slinging her to the floor. Picking up the cell phone he stared at Reeses name on the front screen.

"Just a friend, huh? Let me guess? You working with her too?"

"I don't know what you're talking about, Slick. I'm not working with anyone on anything," she cried while scooting across the floor.

Rushing towards her he delivered a right fist to the side of her head. After she began to scream he ripped the thin tee shirt she was wearing and placed a strong hand around her throat, cutting off all ability to breathe.

"I'm gonna show you exactly why I'm the wrong person to cross," he said with demon like eyes before knocking her unconscious.

***

8:45pm

"Stone, where are you taking me?" Reeses asked curiously. "I've got too much on my mind and too much business to handle to be playing a guessing game."

"Understandable and just like I told you, tonight will be the only night you can relax before it's back to work in the morning. You're straining yourself, you need a break," he stated truthfully, not looking at her hypnotizing grey pupils.

Shaking her head with a small smile, she began to scroll through her phone. After receiving the strange text from Rose earlier, she decided to give her a call. Before the line could ring twice, Stone grabbed it gently from her hands and placed inside his pocket.

"No distractions, just relaxing," he demanded while keeping his eyes on the road.

After twenty minutes of driving he parked the car in front of a local restaurant and stepped out.

"Boy, where the hell are we?"

"You're a very inquisitive girl," Stone laughed before grabbing her hand and heading across the street.

"Inqui- what?"

"It means you're very curious. In other words nosy as hell," he smiled before walking inside.

The smooth eatery looked more exquisite upon stepping in. The waiters moved about from table to table serving the guests, the small jazz band that sat on the stage performed a light tune and the dim lights set the mood for all the couples that entertained each other.

"What is this place?" Reeses asked as Stone led her over to a small table.

"It's an under-rated restaurant for musicians to come and perform their music. No words, just instruments. My mom use to bring me here when I was younger because she said I talked too much and didn't do enough listening. After coming a few times I understood her reasoning."

"And what was that?" Reeses asked with a raised brow.

Crossing his arms he sat back looking before speaking, "Sometimes we spend our life listening to so many words and people that we can't decipher what's real from fake. We worry about the things that don't matter instead of observing the things that are true. For instance, if that was a rap group on stage performing your favorite song, you would probably sing along with the crowd because that what you're used to."

"And what if I just like the song?"

"Exactly. You and the rest of the restaurant. Sometimes people will mimic, react and even try to relive certain things they hear in the mix of music. The same reasons you have children growing up wanting to be a kingpin or maybe even a killer. Words influence people in a way that we will never be able to understand. The most won't catch on until something critical happens, like losing a family member or even worse, their own life. Music was never meant to produce words, only sound. When people began to add their thoughts to instruments they mixed in a few extra things that would change everything."

"A few extra things like what?"

"Pain, emotions, lies, all the things that can pollute your mind to feel a certain way. These are now natural habits that people have adapted to. And it all leads back to hearing bullshit."

"I guess that does make sense," she replied before the water arrived at the table.

After ordering their meal they sat and conversed for the next hour about life goals and future moves to perfect the business. Reeses couldn't help but smile, her heart felt so different at that time. It had been several months since she'd actually enjoyed herself. A lot of things were actually starting to become clear now. If you changed your thoughts you could change the world around you.

"So, what do you think? Do you like it?" Stone asked finishing the last sip of champagne.

"Absolutely, I truly appreciate this. I feel that it was much needed. I think I discovered another part of myself tonight, thanks to you, professor," Reeses replied with a small giggle.

"The innate power you possess to achieve your dreams is immeasurable. When you let go you create space for better things to come into your life, Rinesha."

Taking in his sincere words, she looked deeply into his eyes. "What is it you want from me, Stone?"

"I want you to find happiness. It hurts me to sit back and witness a woman as beautiful as you struggle with people who mean you no good. I would like a chance to show you a better way. An opportunity to show that you are worth loving and that things don't have to be so rough on you," he replied matching her gaze.

Stuttering with her words, she blushed. "People are always sure what they want until they actually have it in their possession, Stone. It's natural for humans to be attracted to each other, but I'm tired of just being a grey-eyed, big booty, young girl with money. My life has navigated towards success whether it was wrong or right decisions I made to see it happen. Love didn't play a position in that and most bitches will only ride with who they think is a winner. I discovered one trait that will be inside of me no matter what. Hustling! Money makes me cum. Control of a multi-million dollar business sends chills through my pussy on a hot and sweaty night. That's a natural love that a woman should feel no matter what."

Standing to her feet, Reeses moved close to him and placed a soft kiss on his cheek. "I think it's time to leave."

Smiling, Stone placed two one hundred dollar bills on the table and moved along her side. His head couldn't wrap around the fact that the woman before him was so young, but filled with tons of knowledge. Her energy along with the amazing beauty she carried was a plus that made him crave for her even more. Regardless of her feelings now, he wasn't going to stop until she was laying in his arms with a ring on her finger.

Chapter 7

Opening his eyes slowly, the sun blurred his vision. His chest felt as if it was on fire and the headache that pumped through his forehead was like a gorilla trying to be released from its cage.

"Salim! Salim, are you okay?" Stone asked as he gradually came to his senses.

Licking his dehydrated lips, he stared at Reeses, Bang and Knox who stood over him with a look of worry.

"Where am I?" he uttered in a dry tone.

"You're in the hospital, Ahkie, you were shot. What the fuck happened?" Stone questioned with anger written all over his face.

Breathing heavily, he closed his eyes. His mind flashed back to Shakur putting the pistol to his face. The threatening words he guaranteed to make happen, the loud bang and bright flash from the gun before everything went black.

"Shakur!" he mumbled.

"I told you he had something to do with this, Stone. You should have never brought him along with us. He's a fucking snake," Reeses raged while looking down at Salim's helpless face.

"Me not want to step in ya business, boss man, but de pussyhole slides on his belly. Him all ova de place. Dead de boy on brush who all behind him," Knox said speaking for the first time.

Pulling out his phone, Stone prepared to dial his number. Grabbing his hand Reeses stopped him quickly.

"There's no more room for talking. We need to find him and end this shit."

"Rent a room and text me where you are. If it's not me, Laylah or Mariah, don't answer," he said before motioning his hand for Knox and Bang to follow him.

***

Super 8 Motel

Snorting another line of cocaine, Slick looked over at Rose's dead body sitting in the corner. The blood from the gruesome slit across her throat had dried and the stench of her released bowels were starting to spread throughout the room.

Watching his phone vibrate, he picked it up and answered, "Who the fuck is this?" he asked with a discombobulating slur.

"It's the woman who's gonna hang you from a tree by your neck in the back of my yard for fucking decoration. I asked you to bring me the girls and it's been almost three days with no word, Mr. Rivers. Is there a problem?" Eva questioned through the receiver.

"Oh, Ms. Deblanco, sorry that things haven't been working on the normal speed that you are used to. I guess I'm too busy worrying about catching a bullet to the face while trying to handle your dirty work."

"You'll be catching more than just a bullet if the deal is not completed, you stupid monkey! I spared your life, a favor for a favor!"

"Sorry, bitch, but the favors have finally run out. I'm a walking death date with or without you. So fuck you and catch me when you can!" he yelled smashing the cell phone into the wall.

The voices of Jimmie and his mother were starting to roam through his head causing him to place his hands over his ears.

"Shut the fuck up talking to me," he screamed, picking up his pistol.

The sound of Rose's phone ringing caused him to jump in a panic. Picking it up from the floor he watched Reeses name flicker across the screen. Licking his lips with a psychotic expression, he answered. Silence spread through the line before she spoke.

"I know it's you, Slick!" I can smell you from anywhere!"

"You just won't stop until I kill everyone you're associated with. I knew she was working with you. So, before I slit her throat I shoved my dick in her ass to make sure you think before sending another one of your friends to set me up, bitch."

He moved the phone from his ear when Reeses began to laugh loudly.

"Rose was never my friend, idiot, she was only a pawn. You're a rapist, your weakness is women. So all that wonderful time you spent butt fucking her corpse will be the reason you die within the next few seconds," she stated with a small chuckle.

Rising to his feet, he quickly gravitated to the door an opened it. The two bullets that flew past his head into the room forced him to hit the floor instantly. Pushing back inside, Slick steadied his weapon before running out and releasing bullets like a mad man.

Boc! Boc! Boc! Boc! Boc! Boc! Boc!

Moving closer to the breezeway of the motel, he fired two more reckless shots before taking cover behind a broken soda machine.

The bullets that Bang released from the semi-automatic carbon 15 shredded throughout the thin medal. The slug that ripped a chunk out of his thigh next is what caused him to yell in tremendous pain before hitting the ground.

"Fuckk!"

Wishing for a blessing, Slick caught his break as an Atlanta patrol car swerved into the parking lot.

Bang wasted no time pushing as many bullets as possible through the driver's side door of the cop car.

As Slick watched him dismember the car piece by piece he took the opportunity and fled towards the back side steps. The blood that was spilling out of him caused his leg to go in and out as he stumbled to keep his balance. Making his way to the Jeep Cherokee, he got inside and shook nervously as he started the engine. Swerving out of the parking space he headed to the front of the motel and spotted Bang aiming the rifle in the street.

"Come on motherfucker!" Slick yelled as he accelerated on the gas pedal and sped directly towards Bang.

Diving out of the way, Bang jumped back to his feet with the quickness and emptied the rest of his clip until the car was out of sight. Bang spat on the ground, his mind was in a rage that he'd actually missed his target. Hotel occupants glared out of their windows and the nearby police sirens forced him to abandon the car and make his way through the woods for a clean getaway. One thing was for sure the next time the two met, Slick wouldn't be so lucky.

***

Northside Hospital 1:30 pm

"I never said I didn't believe you, Stone! But this is our brother you're talking about here. I just can't see him doing something like this without a reason behind it, Ahk," Justin said slowly, sitting up in his bed.

"Reasons like greed, money, hate. You mean shit like that, right? It's Alhamdulilah that you love your brother but he tried to kill Salim and that shit is not about to slide with me."

"So what, you're the executioner now? You're not Allah, nigga! Have any one of you approached the brother or asked what happened from his side of the story or is everyone just moving off their own emotions?"

"Emotions? This dirty ass nigga disappeared into thin air and miraculously your brother ends up shot in this man's living room and you see nothing wrong with that? Are you starting to distrust my word or something? What the fuck is going on with you?" Stone asked with a suspicious eye.

Staring out the glass window, he smirked, "I've been the same person since you met me in prison. I brought y'all into this because I had no choice. I had no one else. Now I'm starting to think I made the wrong decision. All I wanted to do was keep my little sister safe."

"By bringing her into a life of evil? You misled her, Justin. You stood by her side and encouraged her to be the woman she's become and it's finally falling back on you. Maybe you need to evaluate yourself on your own agenda and come back to the light of what we truly believe in, Ahkie."

"What do we believe in, Stone? Because the last time I checked you were the same brother slaying niggas in the street just because. You put on an act as if things have been forgotten, but they aren't. You took people lives for a living and you were proud of that. No one judged you, no one criticized that choice and now you sit in my face and portray yourself to be the best Muslim you can be."

"I'm starting to sense now that this goes beyond our religion, Justin. I've showed you more support than anyone of your fake ass mad dogs could've ever shown. See the problem isn't with everyone else, it's with yourself. You're stuck with the way things are going and you're trying to blame us all for the fumble."

"Nigga, I made myself," he spat, leaning up.

"And that's something that you have to deal with," Stone shot back with a matching attitude.

"Liberty Point," Justin mumbled before crossing his arms.

Hearing the information he needed, Stone made his way out of the hospital room. All his mind could focus on at the time was getting his hands on Shakur.

After turning on the hall towards the elevator, Agent Myers stepped out of the waiting room with her hat pulled low over her eyes. Moving swiftly to Justin's room, she took a deep breath before walking inside and shutting the door behind her.

Chris Green

Chapter 8

Liberty Point Apts. 7:15pm

Before killing the lights to the car Stone grabbed his 45 automatic and Glock 19 from under the driver's seat. His eyes observed the scenery of the quiet complex before he stepped out of the vehicle. While moving swiftly up the sidewalk Stone clutched the guns behind his back as he trailed up the flight of stairs.

***

"Boy, I'm letting you know right now, Shakur, you can't be laying up in here running from them police. This the only time you show yo ass up to my house when you in some damn trouble. All that good ass money you be spending, shoulda been through with paying for a damn mansion by now," the young woman stated, walking into the kitchen.

"Auntie, all I need is a few days and I'm gone. Look at all this illegal shit you got going on in here. Ain't no way you finna start tripping on me," he pointed looking at the four men who gambled in the living room.

Hearing the knock on the front door grabbed his aunt's attention long enough for him to slide to the restroom. Her intentions were to quiet everyone down before opening the door until the barrel of Stone's gun shoved inside of her mouth. Pushing inside of the apartment, he placed a slug into the first man's skull that stood to his feet.

Boc!

Watching the young hustler's brain splatter caused all movements to pause.

"Please don't make me get rid of everyone who's sitting inside this home," Stone said in a quiet and humble manner. "I'm looking for Shakur."

Shaking in fear, the woman looked into Stone's eyes and lied, "I haven't seen him in weeks. He called me yesterday and said that he was in some type of trouble and he would come see me when things were handled. I'm just his aunt," she mumbled in a low voice with tears running down her cheekbones.

Looking around the room at all the silent faces, he tilted his head before opening his mouth. "Your nephew is in very deep trouble. The line that he's crossed could've gotten everyone who is sitting in front of me killed tonight. If you hear from him, if you see him, let it be known that Stone is looking for him and when we cross paths he will die. Do you understand?"

Nodding, she quickly replied, "Yes."

Backing up to the door Stone left just as swiftly as he came. Rushing over to the young man on the floor she eyed Shakur slowly walking out of the bathroom.

"I told you I didn't want you here. What am I suppose to tell his father, Steven?" she yelled calling Shakur by his government name.

Staring down at Hector's dead body, he rubbed a shaking hand over his face.

"Fuck!" he shouted biting on his fist.

Not only was he at war with his Muslim brothers, but the MS-13 gang leader would definitely want answers to why his son wouldn't make it home that night.

"What the fuck are you going to do, Shakur?" she asked while everyone scrambled to get rid of all the drugs in the home.

Grabbing his pistol from under the living room couch, he eyed her with nervousness in his expression.

"I'll handle it, I'm gonna fix it," he assured.

"You better! Cause if you don't, Torez will be coming after you about his son's death, not me," she guaranteed, rocking the seventeen year old back and forth in her lap.

Soaking in her threat, he placed his pistol in the lining of his pants and walked out.

***

Downtown Atlanta

Standing out in the mirador, Reeses glanced out at the illuminating city lights. The life that she'd imagined to be so great was turning out to be her worst nightmare. Trying to imitate a pattern of family tradition was starting to imbalance her mind frame.

Hearing an unfamiliar ringtone on her cell, she looked down at the unknown number with suspicion before picking up.

"Rinesha?"

She heard a woman's voice speak through the line. Feeling her heart race, Reeses knew that one voice that would always be sweet to her ears.

"Auntie Tiffany?" she mumbled just above a whisper.

"How are you?"

Fighting back tears, she held her composure and gave the veracity that was on her heart.

"You leave me for ten years after promising that you would rescue me from this terrible dream and now you ask how am I? I sat up night after night waiting for you to show and you never did. You were all I had left."

"I'm so sorry, baby. Our lives were never meant to be severed apart. I've tried so many times to break you away from the woman who held you captive that it nearly drove me crazy. I searched for you year after year to the point that I thought I failed. Jimmie would have wanted me to have you and I failed him. Your life was suppose to be spectacular, with no worries. I just didn't have enough time, Rinesha, I would never abandon you," Tiffany replied in a sincere tone.

Holding the phone close to her ear, Reeses' eyes welled with tears of pain.

"I know that I can't change what has already occurred, sweetie. I also know that you have grown to be a courageous businesswoman from the things that your cousin Mariah has told me. Please come home, baby. Come to where you truly belong, with your real family."

"I love you but right now I have my own priorities and I'll have to make that decision when the time comes."

"I understand."

Ending the call, she wiped her face before hearing the light knock on her room door. Walking off the balcony, she moved through the suite and glanced out of the peephole. Seeing Stone standing on the other side, she unlocked the latch allowing him to enter.

"Are you okay?" He instantly stopped walking, noticing that her eyes were red.

"I think so," she stated walking towards the large couch and taking a seat.

Attaching the lock in place, he took a seat next to her. "I know there might be a lot of different things bothering you, but faith is all you have as your backbone and you have to keep it strong."

"Sometimes I feel like faith just doesn't exist anymore."

"No matter what you go through never speak that way. You've grown to be an intelligent and quite remarkable young woman. In order to have knowledge you must go through an experience and that's the stage you're at right now. Even though it may not seem like it, a lot of us are going to support you, no matter what. I'm going to stand by your side, right or wrong," Stone assured her with a confident smile.

"Thanks," she replied standing to her feet. "I think I just need some sleep."

Seeing her dim the lights, he stood to leave.

"Don't," she motioned for him to sit back down.

His mind jumbled with confusion as she stood in front of him and released her strapless Versace dress, letting it drop to the floor. Her nipples were chocolate like a Hershey's kiss and her plump womanhood stuck out showing off her delicate lips as if she was in heat.

Swallowing his spit, Stone turned his head. "Reeses what are you doing? Please put back on your clothes, you're naked." He fidgeted like he was breaking the law.

Climbing on top of him, she grabbed his hands placing them on her round, juicy bottom.

"I just want you to hold me, please," she said in a soft voice while burying her face into his neck.

Leaning his head to the side to look in her eyes he took a deep breath, "I need you to say something for me."

"What?"

"Say Lailaha illallah."

"What does that mean?' she asked locking her hands around his neck.

"Please Rinesha, just say it," Stone commanded with love in his eyes.

"Laillaha illallah," she whispered.

Slowly kissing her lips, a single tear fell from his eye as he picked her up, walking towards the bed. Laying her down gently, he shed his clothes.

"I promise I won't hurt you," he mouthed spreading her legs to plant his mouth against her warm pussy lips.

"Please look at me while I please you," he uttered before rolling his tongue around her juicy clit.

"Mmmm!" she moaned grabbing her tittie in satisfaction.

She watched as he massaged up and down her inner thigh while sucking her womanhood into submission.

"Yes," she panted, feeling him slide a finger inside of her.

His mouth was unleashing a feeling that she never felt, jolts of pure pleasure ran through her body. His pace was a mixture of torment and pleasure in the same bundle. After five minutes of running his tongue on her kitty she exploded in an orgasm. Feeling her body lift slightly from the bed Stone locked onto Reeses' pussy as if he was sucking milk from a baby bottle.

"Stone," she gasped.

Turning her over on all fours he mounted her from behind and slowly eased his dick inside of her.

"Oh my Goddd!" she panted feeling his length stretch her out.

Rubbing his large hands down her back he circled around her humongous ass cheeks before spreading them apart, licking her asshole gently. He slowly plunged his rod into her sopping wet pussy. Looking back at him with her dark grey eyes caused him to shove every inch inside of her.

"You feel so good, Rinesha," he grunted, enjoying the back shot of her round ass.

Latching on to her waist she buried her face in the sheets as he sped up his pace. Reeses' back started to arch deeper and her ass clapped loudly while he long stroked her womanhood.

"Shittt! I'm cumming again," she squealed in a light tone while clutching the bed sheet.

"Let it go, baby," Stone growled into her ear as he watched her cream heavily on his member.

Sliding out of her, he laid on his back and guided her on top of him. Turning around she squatted on top of his rod reverse cowgirl style as he held her hips.

His sex was sending her mind to a different planet and now she could feel him climbing deeply into her guts.

"Please, daddy, make me cum again," she begged sliding down on his full length and back to the tip.

The moist sounds of her pussy farting excited Stone causing him to lose control.

"Bounce that ass. Don't play with it, ma," he urged slamming a right hand down on her butt cheek.

"Oooo!" she cried biting her bottom lip.

Massaging her titties, he whispered, "I love you," in her ear before releasing himself.

Catching her breath, Reeses turned around and laid against his chest in silence.

"Did I do too much?" he asked, seeing her face wet from recent tears.

"No, thank you for being my friend, Stone."

Wrapping her in his arms tightly, he caressed her back until she fell into a deep sleep. Even though his heart was happy, his brain couldn't shake the fact that trouble was lying in the streets ready to take them under at any second. Enemies were starting to grow by the day and loved ones were starting to change by night. It was coming to a point where he didn't trust anyone. Regardless of who proved to be working the other side his position would always stand firmly. Protect Reeses until the mission was over with and get her far away from Georgia as possible.

***

West End Clinic

"Sheldon, I don't want to sound harsh but I'm not into this line of work anymore. You might need to go see a professional doctor after this. You've lost a lot of blood," the man said applying the last bandage to his leg.

"What the fuck do you mean you're not in this line of work anymore? You're a fucking doctor, ain't it? What about pills? Prescribe me some medicine," Slick demanded looking around with a crazed expression.

"I have a few anesthetics, but with your injury you're gonna need something much stronger and that can only come from a hospital, Sheldon," the doctor confirmed removing his gloves.

Rubbing his temples with anger, he began to crack his knuckles.

"What about voices? You got anything for that? Something that will make me sleep?"

"Voices?"

"Yes, voices, motherfucker! In my head. Can you give me anything to make it stop?'

"Sheldon, you might need to see a psychiatrist. Voices are something that's uncontrollable. It's a disorder that starts from stress, maybe even guilt. It's more of the intellectual being contrasted with dark emotions. If you don't get help now, it could eventually lead to insanity," the man stated with a serious face.

Standing to his feet, the doctor quickly stepped in front of him.

"Sheldon, I think you need some serious help. I wouldn't recommend you leaving without me calling someone."

Pulling his gun from his waist, he placed it to his chin.

"No phone calls. I don't want to have to come back and see you," he mouthed before walking out of the office.

Chris Green

Chapter 9

"So, what are we looking at?" Stone asked Harvey, the family attorney as he and Reeses occupied the couch inside the hotel room.

"After reviewing all of the State's evidence, we're kind of in a lose-lose situation. The district attorney is trying to bring everything down with the case. First, they have a drug agent that is willing to testify. Usually that wouldn't be a problem with this family because the most don't make it to see the court date, if you get my drift. Unfortunately, she's under the Witness Protection Act and if anything happens from now until that date you might never walk the earth again. Second, the State is trying to tie numerous murder cases to you. Cases that include federal informants, all the way down to people you've dealt with personally. Most of them are beatable. Some are just accusations with no physical evidence."

"And which ones aren't?" Stone asked with a worried expression.

"One. A man named Brandon Kelsey."

"Beno," Reeses admitted, placing her hands over her face.

"Not only that," Harvey continued, "being that the judge is a very unsociable person, it's hard to get a word out of him. On the strength of going to law school with my father, he gave me another piece of information."

"And?" Reeses asked impatiently.

"There's another key witness who's going to be testifying against you at trial."

"Who is it?"

"Now that's what he wouldn't tell me. It seems like they have a few tricks up their sleeves that we weren't prepared for."

"How much time am I truly looking at?" Reeses frowned with sadness.

"Well if we take it to trial and lose, you probably looking at thirty-five to forty years with a possibility of parole.

"What! I've never been arrested a day in my life. I can't do that much time."

"I understand Rinesha, three counts of drug trafficking and four counts of malice murder with a list of other charges that run a mile long will bring numbers like that," Harvey stated truthfully.

"What about a plea deal?" Stone asked.

"If we go for the plea I can guarantee you get no more than ten years may be less."

"I can't do ten years in prison," Reeses mouthed looking at Stone.

"So, there's absolutely nothing else we can do to stop her from doing jail time?"

Thinking before he responded Harvey exhaled deeply, "The only thing that can stop this is if you found out who their surprise witness is and put them in a box including the drug agent who would be nearly impossible to find. It'll be tough to prove that you didn't have anything to do with her coming up missing but I can crumble that cookie if you keep your movements limited in the process. Last but not least, you'll have to break into the district attorney's home and make sure he doesn't make it to work for the next few days. I got the judge to grant us a two week extension on the trial. So whatever you're gonna do, you better hurry."

"It'll be handled," Stone assured in a stern tone.

"Well, I guess I'll see you all at trial, good luck," Harvey replied grabbing the briefcase off the table and heading for the door.

Sensing the worry spilling from Reeses' aura, Stone sat next to her placing a hand on her leg.

"Listen, it's going to be okay. I'm not going to let this happen to you. Even if I gotta place a bullet in the judge's head, my damn self. You may need to go see Justin one last time because if it comes down to it and things are looking shaky. We getting you the fuck out of the United States. You have more than enough money and you'll be safe in the islands with your family."

"And what about everyone else?" she asked with a genuine attitude.

"That's something that everyone will have to decide when the time presents itself. I don't care what everyone else wants to do. I'll follow you around the world if you want me to," he replied squeezing her hand gently.

After kissing her lips passionately, they both prepared to head out and complete a deadly task that would take a miracle from Allah not to fail.

***

Pulling up to the humongous home, Frost parked her burgundy Aston Martin DBII next to her mother's black Masarati Levante S and stepped out. It was almost twelve o'clock in the evening and the drizzling rain was starting to pour harder as she made her way inside.

Upon entering the home, she unbuttoned her Moncler Arriette coat and tossed it on the floor. Her reddish hair hung freely down her back, her white Valentino jeans hugged her slim frame matching the Garvanni heels that clicked against the floor tile as she moved through the elegant residence.

Walking into the giant living space she observed her Aunt Eva who sat quietly sipping on a glass of orange pekoe tea with a cigarette between her fingers,

"It was once said by a wise woman that control can only be enforced upon someone that's willing to be tamed. Now ain't that bout a bitch," she smiled, while looking down at the newspaper in front of her.

Smiling, Frost crossed her legs. "No one wants to be controlled, auntie. That's the reason you have authority. To ensure that they don't have a choice."

"How are you, darling?" she asked focusing her attention on Frost.

"I'm bored. Spending money is starting to become very dull and I think my mother is relapsing from the bullet again."

"She's not relapsing. Her mind is just permanently frightened from your father."

Sipping her tea, she shook her head in disgust. "He's the fucking devil reincarnated. All three of your uncles and your papa are dead because of him. I know that motherfucker is still alive. It's like I can smell his scent roaming through the city of Atlanta as we speak."

"Maybe it's a gift and a curse, Auntie. This family has an oral history. We were marked for destruction and chaos, it's in our nature. God has sent a way for us to build what you would call a legacy and it's going to end with us holding the torch," Frost stated holding her arm in the air.

"Indeed we will, my sweetheart."

"Not to rain on your parade but I think your agent puppet has exposed our hand, the mission was to leave people clueless but I'm starting to hear a lot of news being spread."

"Smith is only a source for now. If things get out of control I'll let you take over."

"They know about everything, Eva! While we've been sitting back wasting time on killing these bitches, your stupid servant has gone out there and exposed our entire hand. This mishap is going to lead the Feds directly to our door or even worse to my fucking mother. Since I was a young girl you showed me how to be a killer. Not just any killer but a smart one. We never leave a trail and there is never room for any mistakes. Remember?" Frost mentioned to refresh her aunt's memory.

Standing up, she moved closer to the enormous fireplace savoring the heat.

"I've never been perfect, darling. My goal was to outlast all competition and get revenge on the ones who hurt us the most. We've never moved off speculations or feelings."

"My feelings died the day I was born and speculating something is the fastest way to get everyone murdered on a humbug. I'm stating facts. The cop has to go, Eva. There's no other way."

"Understood. I'll deal with it my darling and after we settle the score you can go out and have the fun you've been waiting for," Eva assured with a smile.

***

Brooklyn, New York
Patsy's Italian Restaurant

Ignoring Reeses phone call for the third time, Laylah stepped out of the New York taxi with a complete makeover. The blonde wig and glasses she wore gave her the look of a thirty year old librarian. The black expensive Michael Kors dress squeezed her plump backside showing off all of her seductive curves and the large Gucci pocketbook that hung across her shoulder complimented the slide in Burberry heels that showed her toes.

"If you don't mind, sir, I'll only be a second. Five minutes tops," she said handing the old white man a crisp hundred dollar bill.

"Sure thing, sweet cakes," he replied watching her ass move loosely.

Strutting to the entrance she made her way inside and glanced around before a male server approached her.

"Good evening, ma'am. Is there any way I can be of assistance to you?"

"Yes, you may. Table for two and if you don't mind I would like you to tell Mr. Lucca that Ms. Korperman is here to see him."

"Absolutely. Right this way." He moved smoothly to a secluded section for her to sit. "Can I offer you anything to drink?" he asked.

"No. thank you, I won't be long," Laylah replied, placing her purse on the table.

Heading to complete her request, she waited patiently until Saul made his way out of the kitchen area. Adjusting his tie, he walked with a slight limp over to Laylah's table.

"Ms. Koperman! It's a pleasure to finally meet you," he greeted with a thick Italian accent. Besides the splotches of grey hair he still looked the same as he did sixteen years ago.

"The pleasures all mine, Mr. Lucca. I've came quite some way to do business with you. I hope that I'm not intruding on your schedule," Laylah said in a sweet tone.

"No, not at all. My boss wants you to know that all prices are still the same that we spoke about on the phone."

"Good."

Pulling a small photo from her pocketbook she slid it across the table towards him.

"Do you recognize that woman?"

Glancing down at the photo, he looked at Laylah with confusion written on his face.

"I don't recall," he lied instantly having a flashback.

"Sure you do," Laylah replied, quickly pulling the Glock 17 with a compressor from the purse with expertise.

Choking on his words, she refreshed his memory, "Sixteen years ago you helped kidnap my stepmother from my father and held her for ransom for a man named Pauly. Today that very consequence has cone to haunt you. Just like Ghost," Laylah smiled before the trigger six times.

Watching him crumble to the floor, she left Erica's picture face up on the table before exiting the restaurant. Stepping back into the cab, she handed the man another C-note.

"Back to the airport, please."

"Right away, ma'am."

***

Northside Hospital

Walking inside Justin's hospital room, she stared at him lying on the bed. Eyes closed with his arms folded. Closing the door she moved to his side and took a seat on the bed next to him.

"Wassup, little one," he groaned stirring out of a fake sleep as if he didn't know she came in.

"Hey, are you feeling better?" she asked, truly concerned.

"Don't have much of a choice. I'm starting to regain the feeling in my back again. What about you? Why the long face?"

"There's a lot going on out here, Justin. Harvey said that I might be facing jail time when I go to trial."

Sensing his mood change, he used his hands to sit up.

"What do you mean?"

"From the evidence the state has on me. He said that's there's no way I can win. The D.A. is even finding secret witnesses to testify against me along with Courtney."

"Do you know a name?" he questioned anxiously.

"No, Harvey said the judge isn't budging on anything. This shit is going terribly wrong and it's starting to scare me. I still have the last supply of twenty keys that I took from Chi. Maybe we should just get rid of it all and leave," Reeses suggested.

"Leaving is not on my mind right now, Rinesha. What about everything we built? You can't just tell me you're willing to turn your back on all this. Not to mention the drama we have going on in the streets that's unfinished."

"Justin, all that shit amounts to nothing. I was talking to Stone and"

"Stone?" he spat cutting her off. "Is that who put you up to this? He was only suppose to protect you, Rinesha. Not play under you. Maybe you need to start with getting the hell away from him," he raged on more of a personal note.

"Justin, I have over sixteen million dollars stashed in three overseas accounts. We can start over. There's nothing personal about spacing ourselves as far as possible from this bullshit. What don't you understand about that?"

"This is us, Reeses. No matter where we run, no matter how far we go, we still gonna be the Rivers' family. It's in our blood, sis. Our siblings and close relatives have died standing behind this."

"Exactly and I'm not gonna make that list to be in a fucking box behind them. I'm telling you ahead of time if that trial starts to look funny, I'm leaving, with or without you. You're the only brother I have left, Justin and I don't wanna lose you. The time has come to decide which is more important. Living up to a name or keeping our lives to live another day with each other," she stated before walking out of the room.

Chapter 10

Walking into the Federal building downtown, Courtney made her way to the third floor D.E.A. unit. Knowing that she was breaking a protocol for being on the premises she kept her head low until reaching her superior's office.

Knocking lightly his voice could be heard from the other side. "Come in."

Cracking the door, Courtney slid inside closing it behind her. "Sir?"

Looking at her he removed his glasses with a stern expression.

"Myers, what the hell do you think you're doing? I gave you permission to go active, not to pop up on the work site. If someone sees you, I can lose my job," he stated seriously.

"Sir, I am so sorry, but I think that we have something bigger on our hands and if we don't get a hold of it right now we might be too late later on."

His nose flared with anger as he motioned for her to sit down.

"Let me explain something to you. The procedures for witness protection is to guarantee that our own are protected by any means. You're risking a lot by sitting in this office right now. So, whatever you have to say it damn sure better be good."

"When you first assigned me to this case a year ago, I dug deeply into observing this family. Now if you remember, Mr. Grey was the outcast of the relatives which started a chain reaction of the chaos we have on our hands today. According to the documents you gave me, the suspect had relations with an agent named Erica Harper who eventually went rogue on the government. The last time she was spotted was sixteen years ago boarding a private jet in New York with the fugitive. Moving forward to his aunt, her name is Eva Ramirez, the daughter of the notorious crime boss Jesus Ramirez aka "The God". After rumors spread of the suspect murdering his grandfather in cold blood, she took over all of her father's assets, accounts and businesses. Including supplying cocaine to a small portion of the United

States. Her connections stretched widely from paid politicians, governors and even agents of the Bureau."

Sitting back in his chair he placed a hand on his chin as she continued to spill the information.

"Now the case that's about to take place involving Rinesha Rivers is closer than you think. Her father Jimmie Rivers, who is now deceased, has a sister that goes by the name of Tiffany Reid. Can you guess who she's been suspected of having ties with?"

"Mr. Grey," he answered correctly.

"Exactly. She signed her name for him as his wife for a bond on a massive shooting case that took place in Mozley Park. Out of the small time that Ms. Rivers involved me into her business you had three deaths occur with law enforcement officials including my father who was investigating her also. Now a while back Ms. Ramirez lost three sons to a tragic death by the hands of Mr. Grey once again. Things then became more personal."

"I would appreciate it if you stop being vague and get to the point, Agent Myers."

"Their history is built off killing relatives and according to the FBI, Ms. Ramirez has been sliding her way around Atlanta, Georgia for the past few weeks. I think she's planning to kill Rivers."

"Now that sounds good but how does she know about Rivers if they aren't immediate family? The information could only come from research through authorities."

"Which can only mean one thing, sir."

"A dirty cop," he mouthed.

"Exactly," she smiled.

Picking up his office phone he pointed a finger at her. "I don't want you taking this head on by yourself, Myers. This is beyond serious. If we can stop this it'll be the biggest case of the century for this department. Stay clear and move silently until this is over," he commanded.

"Yes sir," she replied, heading for the door.

Little did he know she already had the valuable information that he truly needed.

***

Kennesaw, Ga.

"Regardless of how your brother feels he's not in a position to speak on this matter, Rinesha. If your court date is in two weeks that means we need to start knocking pieces off this chess board."

"Obviously I get that. My question is how can I do that when everyone is all over the place. I don't have eyes in the back of my head, Mariah. If I was the fucking oracle then my problems would've been dead yesterday. Not to mention the so called family situation with this Frost person," she stated while Bang and Stone stood behind her.

"Frost is none of your concern. You may have earned a living with pushing product, but I gained a reputation for the art of war. When she shows her face she will perish at that exact second. Let me be clear when I say this, we are not a normal family and never will be. My father along with yours did the things they had to in order for us to shine differently from others. Take a look around, Rinesha. None of this came from the average thinker. Since my father has been dead, my mother has run this operation with an iron fist. Now the torch will soon be handed to us."

"And you say this because?"

"I say it because you need to wake the hell up! Your brother, those so called loved ones, you need to wipe that out of your heart. You were made to be the boss of an organization and it's time to start thinking like one. I've sent six men on the hunt for these two imbeciles that've been playing this ridiculous game of cat and mouse with you. It leaves less room to even breathe wrong. If you stop chasing them and think like the queen that you are, their heads will fall directly in your lap," she guaranteed before taking a swig of her champagne.

"She's right. From now on we'll move on our own. There's no sense in risking you to get in more trouble than you're already in. With the help of her guards, Bang and Knox, it's no way we wouldn't be able to find these clowns," Stone agreed.

"You say that now, but you don't know who you're truly dealing with," Reeses warned.

Kneeling in front of her, he grabbed her hand. "You gotta trust me on this one. Even though I hate to admit it, your time for beating your feet is up, baby girl. I don't give a damn what I got to do to end this shit before your court date comes. I don't want you running around and always having to look over your shoulder because we couldn't beat the police at their own game. Shakur and Slick is going to die, Courtney and whoever is working with her will get the same. I'll send Bang to handle the district attorney. Nothing is gonna stop you from walking out of that courtroom. I love you too much for that," he mumbled, staring into her eyes.

"I hope so," she replied matching his gaze.

***

The afternoon was quickly turning into nightfall as Agent Smith pulled his black tinted window Tahoe truck into Eva's parking lot. After getting the call yesterday about their urgent meeting, he made it his business to stop everything he was doing. Walking past the heavily armed guards he strolled into the house. His eyes quickly scanned around and landed on Frost who sat in deep conversation on her cell phone.

"I'm here for your Aunt, is she in?" he whispered.

Pointing upstairs, she returned her attention to the person on the other end of her line. Shrugging his shoulders, he made his way up the large circular staircase that led to the second floor of the massive home. His eyes couldn't help but glance at the large, expensive paintings that hung on the wall as he moved through the hallway.

Reaching the master suite of the home, he knocked lightly and entered. The large room looked more like an apartment than a bedroom. The seventy inch flat screen that was mounted over her balcony door played an episode of the Sopranos at a quiet volume. The dim lights gave the feeling that it was ten o'clock at night instead of seven thirty and the stereo that sat in the corner crooned 'Because You Loved Me" by Celine Dion through the speakers.

Agent Smith walked toward the double doors that would take him to the other side of her partitioned space.

Eva sat on the edge of her queen size bed wearing nothing but a silk garment that was loose. Her perfect C-cup titties sat straight up flaunting her light pink nipples. Her smooth thick legs were crossed exposing nothing but the small layer of neatly trimmed hair that sat over her pussy.

"I can come back if you want me to," he said, lusting with his eyes as they roamed up and down her body.

Sipping her glass of Crème de Cacao, Eva laughed lightly and reached for her pack of Camel cigarettes. After adding fire to the end of one she exhaled before speaking.

"It's kinda hard not to dislike someone like you. Luckily I'm so much of a warm and gentle person that I can withstand that urge."

"Should I take that as a compliment or an insult," he shot back with a smile.

Eva disregarded the smart remark, her expression grew serious. "It seems that a lot of unwanted attention has been making a direct path back to my home. When you first met me I guaranteed that I would keep you under the radar with doing any business with this family. Even personal business. As the days grow old, you still have yet to tell me the hold up on getting the girls to me."

"Listen, Eva, you have to learn a little patience. Your name is on a chart for the FBI and I've kept you brushed under the rug for a very long time now. Just because I work for you doesn't mean that I don't have a job to do. As I've told you before, I need you to stay clear and keep your hands clean until I can complete the job," he stated, trying to put her at ease.

Pulling on her cigarette, she flicked the ashes.

"When I was younger my father promised things that I still don't have to this day. Do you know what that taught me? Not to trust anything a punta motherfucker told me!" she mumbled through slanted lips. "I trust you, which is the only reason you are in my presence or my home. There's a powerful meaning behind lucrative business, Gregory. It's to prosper and grow, but if I have a problem out there in the streets it slows down everything."

"And your words aren't falling on deaf ears, Eva. You say you trust me, but do you? I fight and kill on the strength of you and because I want to. Feels more like I belong here, rather than being needed. The problem has been prolonged enough and it's officially about to end, but let's get something clear. You don't run me nor am I a slave for your organization. I make myself very useful by cleaning up your mess because that's what I enjoy doing. My advice just for future reference, don't be so quick to piss on the ones who're willing to bend over backwards for you at any time," he addressed with a wink and a smile.

Smirking at his arrogance she mashed her cigarette butt into the ashtray. Licking her index finger she opened her legs exposing the chunky lips of her sweet spot. Spreading it apart, her eyes met his with a sexual gaze.

"Only little boys take things to heart, Gregory. What else are you useful for?" she asked with a raised eyebrow.

Rubbing his chin with an amused smile, he slowly moved towards the bed until he stood in between her legs.

"And grown women know how to ask for what they want."

Smoothing his fingers through her hair, she released his zipper and pulled his manhood close to her mouth.

"Shut the fuck up and let a real woman do her job," Eva replied, before slowly deep throating him.

Gregory threw his head back in satisfaction he placed his hand behind her neck. Her pace began to speed up, soaking his manhood with saliva from her warm lips and tongue. Moaning loudly, she slid her hand across his rock hard six pack and started to gag on his rod.

"Damn, Eva," he grunted, looking down into her light brown eyes. "Slow down, mami."

Ignoring his wishes, she started to massage her kitty and moved her lips to the tip of his rod twirling her head from side to side. He couldn't help but force it all back down her throat and release his semen.

"Mmmhmm!" she panted, moving her fingers faster across her clit until she swallowed every last drop.

"Fuck," he whispered before she released him from her mouth.

Lying back on the bed, she spread her legs and pointed to her pussy throbbing for pleasure. Getting on his knees he started to plant kisses on her inner thighs and swirled his tongue around her anus.

"Oh my," she smiled in delight.

"You're not the only one who's grown," he teased before diving headfirst on her pussy hole.

Using his fingers to keep her lips apart, he snapped into a licking frenzy, as if it were his last feast. He knew that he was hitting the right spots after hearing Eva utter words in Spanish under her breath. His mind was so focused on making her cum that he never saw her pull the chrome 380 automatic from under the sheet.

Bloc! The gun erupted loudly, sending a slug through the top of his head, killing him instantly.

Wiping the blood from her face, she grabbed her cigarettes and sparked one. Exhaling, she stared down at his lifeless body.

"Now that was some dangerous oral sex," she said to herself before forcing a small laugh.

Coming around the corner with her Glock 40 in hand, Frost stared at Eva who sat on top of the blood soaked sheets.

"Hey, baby girl," she said as if all was normal.

Throwing on her robe, she stepped over Smith's body until she was face to face with her niece.

"You waited so patiently to play. Now the ball's in your court, my princess," Eva confirmed, while taking another pull of her nicotine.

Wiping the small spots of blood from her forehead, she smiled and placed a kiss on her cheek.

"Thank you, Auntie."

Chris Green

Chapter 11

After making the decision to stay on the prowl for Slick and Shakur without Reeses being involved, Stone made it his business to quickly switch vehicles. He knew the only way to catch a rat was to be sneaky like one. Atlanta was filled with a lot of talkers and word was getting around that absurd drama was stirring up between the Muslim brothers.

Getting the phone call from Wild twenty minutes ago, he was heading out to meet up. Even though Courtney was still well and alive, the media was still broadcasting his face and name on air as if he killed the President. What was even crazier to Stone was how they continued to portray that she was dead and reiterated to the world that Wild was a Muslim terrorist who was paid to perform the malicious act. In their mind that was called positive law, which was basically a ruling established by the government to do what the fuck they wanted.

The worse part about it was many people actually quarreled with the idea of petitioning to get all who represented the Islamic religion out of the United States. Regardless of how much it bothered him, he was only one man with one speech and that just wasn't enough when it came down to fighting the political society.

Pulling down on Pryor St. in front of the Fulton County courthouse, he killed his lights and looked around nervously. It was kind of hard to believe Wild wanted to meet at that location when he was practically the most wanted in Atlanta.

Looking through the rear-view Stone watched the bright headlights of a gray Range Rover pull in behind him and cut off the engine. Holding his pistol in hand, he relaxed after seeing his little brother step out of the vehicle and walk towards his car. Hitting the locks, Wild got in and closed the door behind him.

"As-Salamu-laikum," Stone greeted.

"Wa-laikum as-Salam. How are you, big bro?" Wild asked with a brotherly handshake.

"I'm trying to continue pushing day by day, little brother. Things have been extremely rough since you've been away. Salim was shot and he's in the hospital barely functional."

"What the fuck happened?"

"Shakur," Stone replied, shaking his head.

Rubbing a hand over his face, Wild fought to control his anger. "He was never supposed to be back around us from the jump, bro. The nigga's a fucking dirty wolf in sheep's clothing."

"Trust me, I've been pushing to expose that shit to everyone, Muslim or not. He harmed a brother for a slime ass cause. He can make as many prayers and dua's that he desires. When I catch him, he's gonna die, period. It's even more urgent to get your brother Justin to realize what the fuck we're saying," Stone mentioned, while keeping an eye on their surroundings.

"Speaking of the snake," Wild said in more of a disappointed tone.

"What? What are you talking about?"

Handing Stone the large manila envelope, he pulled a rolled blunt from his ear.

"Look for yourself."

Pulling the thick bundles of paper out, he eyes landed on a picture of Reeses. Slowly reading the small amount of information, Stone started to turn pages, observing the photographs of himself and the rest of their crew. He stopped on Justin's background report. Blinking his eyes repeatedly, he looked back at the paper to make sure he wasn't tripping. The words Federal Informant sat above his picture in bold letters.

"What the fuck is this?"

"Exactly what it says. That nigga Justin's a fucking rat. The documents are attached to the back."

Flipping the page, Stone began to read the statements.

"Before he was released from the Feds, they indicted him on a murder charge for a woman named Margaret Myers. Obviously he knew they weren't bullshitting because he worked a deal with the DEA to help build a case against Reeses. Now it started to make sense why the nigga was always nervous on being around the bitch Courtney. Not only did he know the hoe from when they were younger, she came to see the nigga before he got out to ensure that he would comply with the case. He knew that he couldn't just move around in the streets alone with his sister selling work. So, he needed some fall guys and that's when we came into play. He's been setting us up the entire time, bro," Wild stated while inhaling the weed.

Stone couldn't even feel his heartbeat as his brother filled him in on the critical information. All the love and trust that he carried inside for Justin was officially ripped out and was washed away. Not only was he plotting on the men he called his brothers, but he was working to see his own sister's demise.

"Where did you find this?"

"It was in the back of the bitch's trunk. I just so happen to go through it before I stripped her shit down and sold it. I don't know what everybody else is planning to do, but I'm about to get the fuck back out of the state of Georgia until y'all make it to another location. I hate to see shit go down like this, but I came way up here to deliver this so you can put that girl on point. I know y'all close and it's none of my business. I just feel that you're the only one who can break this to her. If you ask me, he shouldn't be walking the earth the next time I meet up with you guys," Wild said, stepping out of the car.

Thinking to himself, Stone truly wondered what would drive a person to cross the same people that would lay down and die for them. He knew that there were no limitations to greed and someone who desiring to be on top, but looking down at Justin's statements it didn't add up to either of the two. No matter what his intentions were, it was a guarantee that he wouldn't live long enough to see it happen.

***

Southside of Atlanta
Cleveland Ave. 11:45 pm

Standing inside the double wide trailer park home, Torez held the huge machete across his shoulder as he stood in the unrecognizable man's face. The man's hands were chained behind his back and his body was posted against a thick block of wood that was mounted in the center of the floor.

"Where is my money, Vato?"

"Torez, I never cross you, man. You know I would never disrespect our friendship. On my daughter's life," the man pleaded as he breathed harshly.

"Your daughter is like my daughter. I pay for her Christmas, I have picked her up on weekends and spent thousands on her shopping. I even make sure she gets home from school safely. I've been good to you, man," he said with wide eyes, lowering the machete.

"Please, Torez! You have to believe me, man."

Stuffing the dirty sock into the man's mouth, he shook his head.

"I go with my instincts, senor. Unfortunately I don't agree," he said, before grabbing his right hand and disconnecting it from his body.

Even though his horrific screams were being contained by the cloth, the veins that protruded from his face and neck showed the pain that was surging through his body.

Turning around to face the heavily armed men who stood behind him, he tossed the severed hand on the floor.

"The entire trailer park belongs to me. I feed every last one of you daily and all I ask is that my money is correct when I come to collect it, homes. Stealing is above breaking the rules, so I shouldn't have to be here when the problem needs to be handled. Does everybody fucking understand?"

As the men nodded in unison, a sharp knock on the door erupted. Moving quickly, one of the guards opened it allowing the men to enter.

"Hey, Torez, somebody is here to speak with you," the Mexican announced before Shakur stepped in the trailer.

"You got some big fucking nuts coming out here anyway," Torez said with death in his eyes.

His henchmen wasted no time aiming their AK-47s at the center of Shakur's head.

"Please, Torez, I promise whatever you've been hearing isn't true. It's the reason why I came to explain what happened myself," he replied in a fearful tone with his hands in the air.

"Do tell," Torez motioned for his guard to close the door.

***

Grady Memorial Hospital 8:30am

"Are you sure this is the right one?" Frost asked Eva's personal bodyguard as he sat in the driver's seat.

"Yes ma'am, I'm positive. It's the same guy from the pictures," he confirmed in a dark and raspy tone.

"Good. How do I look?" she asked with a sinister smile, while smoothing out the white nursing scrubs.

"You look like a professional doctor, boss," he replied knowing what she wanted to hear.

Observing herself in the mirror once more, Frost stepped out of the black Suburban and headed towards the entrance. Placing her honey blonde hair into a ponytail, she finished off her appearance with a pair of clear lens Ray-Bans.

Judging from the way she moved you would think that she was a jolly Harvard University graduate instead of a psychopathic killer. After taking a look at the guide map, she headed up to the third floor. Her mind was focused on the mission that was ahead of her until a hand reached out and grabbed her shoulder.

Instincts said to reach for the pistol that rested on the small of her back until she turned to face a man wearing a white overcoat.

"Hi, I'm Doctor Cooper. And you are?" he asked holding out his hand.

Catching her off guard she stumbled over her words trying to think of a response.

"Wait, let me think. You're the new intern from Michigan, right?"

"Yes! How did you just guess that?" she asked slashing a fake, cheesy smile.

"It's normal. Anyway, I'm the lead doctor over the hospital. New students have a class on the first floor that starts at ten. I'll see you there," he said, with a wink before walking off.

Moving along she rushed to make her way through the double doors. Her mind was grateful for having patience because if the doctor said the wrong thing his brains would've been plastered on the hallway walls and her entire mission would've been ruined.

The busy area full of nurses gave the perfect distraction as she walked room to room, glaring inside. Just as she thought that Eva's incompetent guard had given her the wrong information, she peeped through the next window and spotted Salim laying peacefully on the hospital bed.

Looking behind her, Frost entered the room letting the door close behind her. The only sounds that lingered in the air were the monitor showing his heartbeat and blood pressure. Walking towards him, she placed her hand on his leg, sliding it slowly up to his crotch.

"It always tingles my pussy to kill a good looking man like yourself. Just for the record, this has nothing to do with you, it's just family business," she whispered into his ear before pulling the syringe out of her pocket.

Bending down she removed the top and slid the needle full of toxic poison inside of the IV tube that was connected to his arm. Watching his chest heave in an upward motion she quickly pushed the fluids into his system.

Stepping back she looked at the uncomfortable expression spread across his face. Placing the small note at the bottom of his bed his heart rate monitor began to alarm.

"Don't fight it, boy, you can't cheat death," she said coldly before leaving out of the room.

Making her way back to the elevator, she knew her job was completed after hearing the code sound off through the intercom. Seeing the nurses run down the hall, she headed to cause torment on her next victim.

Chapter 12

Stepping through the hotel room door, Stone carried the hot breakfast plates in his hand as he walked towards the large bed. Looking down at Reeses sleep, he couldn't help but smile. There was something about the fascinating woman before him that he couldn't get enough of. Her long black hair, the light chocolate skin that always glowed to perfection, her deep and attractive grey eyes that always seem to wrap him in a trance, all these things held his heart.

Sitting the food on the bed, he leaned over her amazing body and planted a kiss on her cheek.

"Good morning and happy birthday," he whispered before placing another on her soft lips.

Smiling, she leaned up staring down at the bags that sat at her feet. "What is all this?"

Pulling a medium size jewelry box from the bag, he handed it to her and stood back in silence. Looking at him with a curious face she opened it slowly and gasped.

After picking up the sparkling diamond bracelet, she stared down at the heart that was once split into two pieces.

"I thought I lost it," Reeses mumbled nearly dropping tears.

"I know how important your mother was to you so I figured, why not piece them together so they could never separate again," he mentioned before clamping it on her wrist.

"Thank you, I love it," she confirmed, hugging his neck tightly.

"You're very welcome. Now you need to eat before your breakfast gets cold. You got steak, scrambled cheese eggs, omelets and hot caramel coffee," he spoke in a funny voice while pulling everything out of the bags.

"Why you being so nice to me? Is this something you really doing from your heart or is it just because I got some good booty?" she giggled with her arms folded.

"Of course it's from my heart, ma and no it's not just because you got some good nooky. This little time we've spent going through these differences in the street has pulled me so close to you. I don't know it feels like I was meant to find you. A man can easily run around and have relations with numerous of women and it still carries no significance. I'm right here because I truly want to be," he assured flashing his perfect thirty-two.

Hearing the knock on the room door, Stone made his way over to answer it. Opening it up, Laylah made her way inside with a huge smile.

"It's your birthday, bitch! Where are we going? Museum, Fern Bank, Aquarium?"

"The Fern Bank?" Reeses repeated before laughing. "I was thinking more on the border line of sticking to the business we need to handle. I know it's supposed to be a so called special day, but if I don't get these priorities in order I'll be spending the next ten birthdays in a prison cell," she said standing out of the bed.

"That's only if we allow it to happen. You're starting to sound too much like Mariah."

"Tell me about it. It's like her power struck voice is stuck inside of my fucking head."

Hearing his cell phone ring, Stone pulled it out of his pocket and stepped out on the balcony.

"Look, forget what everyone else is saying. If you want this handled we're gonna have to get out there and do it ourselves. No one can magically predict where these assholes will be but you. The longer we sit here and wait will be the reason we receive nothing but excuses on why they aren't dead yet."

"Try telling your sister that," Reeses said, shaking her head.

"Listen, when it comes to things I have to handle, I lend an ear to Mariah's words and keep it pushing. She doesn't know everything. Everybody's agenda isn't the same, Rinesha. When you start trying to handle situations like the next person instead of yourself, you lose track of your own purpose."

Before she could reply, Stone walked back into the room with a distraught look on his face.

"Salim is gone," he uttered in a hurt tone.

"What? What do you mean he's gone?" Reeses asked, feeling her body stiffen.

"The doctors at Grady said he died this morning."

"That doesn't make any sense, Stone. The doctors just told us that he would be okay."

"It's definitely strange. If it was a possibility that he wouldn't make it, you guys would've been the first to know. Something doesn't sound right about that," Laylah said.

"Justin is not going to be able to handle this. We may need to move him."

"He's not going to care," Stone said with his head down. His heart was still locked on being the best brother he could but the betrayal from Justin was a secret he refused to hold back from her.

"What the hell would make you say something so stupid? Justin loves Salim, just as much as you do," Reeses said with anger flowing through her body.

Instead of replying to her, Stone moved over to the couch and pulled the manila envelope from under his jacket. It was never his intention to pit a sister against her brother, but his hands were tied. Either she would know the truth or continue to have love in her heart for rat.

Stone walked over to Reeses, he placed it directly into her hands.

Glaring at him with hostility in her eyes, she pulled the thick bundle of papers from the folder. Standing up, Laylah came to stand beside her as she looked at the picture of Ghost.

"That's my dad. Where did you get this?" Reeses asked staring at Stone.

Keeping his silence, the girls continued to fumble through the paperwork in amazement. Reeses heart crumbled when she got to Justin's profile. Although she believed the words Federal Informant had to be wrong, she began to read the pages that followed. After scanning through half of the papers, her hands began to tremble. Reeses watery eyes told the hurt she felt inside as she viewed the statements of Justin willing to turn her in for his own freedom.

"Is this true?" she asked in a weak voice, looking up at Stone.

"I'm sorry, baby girl. I felt you deserved to know," he replied watching the tears drop down her face.

"Rinesha, you need to send someone to get rid of him. He's clearly the witness that your lawyer is warning you about," Laylah stated truthfully.

"No, I'm going to confront him, then I'm gonna kill him myself," she spat with venom and hatred from the heart.

Justin was always that one person she could never lose love for. He was the brother that was supposed to stand behind her through the toughest storms, no matter how hard or rough things got for them. Mariah's cold words ran through Reeses's brain as she grabbed her pistol from under the pillow.

"Your brother, those so-called loved ones, you need to wipe that out of your heart. You were made to be the boss of an organization and it's time to start acting like one."

She now understood the meaning of Mariah's ways. The streets were going to be heartless no matter how much love you showed to them. Everyone was out to stay on top and that was by any means. Even if it meant crossing family. Unfortunately that would be a mistake that Justin would regret forever.

***

Northside Hospital

Making their way inside of the medical center, Reeses stepped on the elevator first, with Stone and Laylah directly behind her.

"Listen, Rinesha, I know you're mad but you still gots to remember we're in a public hospital. If you shoot him, the police will be on us before we can make it back out of this building," Laylah warned.

Even though her temper was boiling through the roof, Reeses knew that Laylah's words were logical.

"Just keep calm, ma. If he tries to deny it, show 'em the paperwork and we can go from there," Stone said, as the doors opened to the fourth floor.

Strolling around to the room, Reeses was the first to enter.

"No fucking way," Stone said, stepping in behind her.

"I think he may have gotten the memo a little earlier than expected," Laylah said looking inside of the empty room.

The medical devices down to the bed sheets were changed and moved.

Walking to the nurse's desk, Reeses stopped the first woman she laid eyes on.

"Yes, how can I help you all?" she asked looking at all three of them curiously.

"My brother, Justin Rivers, he was in room six. Where is he?"

"I don't recall that name," she said typing on the computer in front of her.

"I think we need to get the fuck outta here. Something feels weird," Stone said getting paranoid.

"There's no record of a person with that name ever being here, sweetheart. I'm sorry," the woman assured her before getting back to her duties.

"It's true, he's really about to pull this shit," Reeses said walking off with worry written on her face.

"Just like I told you earlier, it's time to start thinking a little smarter. We have to start getting rid of some of these problems. He's not gonna be able to go far," Laylah said, trying to make sense of the situation.

"Justin has just played himself into the worst predicament ever. I got a plan, you might not like it, but I think it'll work," Stone said with a sly smirk.

***

Federal Headquarters
Downtown, Atlanta

"According to the Bureau, Smith has been missing in action for the past few days. Now that coincides with what we have on our agenda, but I'm afraid it's not enough. We have to catch him in the act, Myers."

"You're right, sir. That's why I had Plan B inside of the chamber. When Smith showed up to the Witness Protection home, his motive was to get me to abandon the trial on the Rivers case. It was like he was sent by someone personally. Not only that," she said digging inside of the beige flip folder.

Sliding the photographs towards him, superior McKenny removed his glasses to get a better view.

"When I requested to continue the case, sir, I began to follow Smith around for the next few days. I made sure to keep a low profile and this is what I came up with. He made over three stops to this large home out in Macon, Georgia. Kind of strange for an agent to be at a residence filled with heavily armed Spanish men guarding the front gate. Whoever they are must have expensive taste because every car in their driveway cost over a hundred grand. Now I don't wanna go outta my league, sir, but you have a major distributing queen pin who happens to be down here in search of blood for a family situation.

The same woman who has paid authorities over ten million dollars in US funds to keep her face golden. Now Agent Smith has happened to find a set of friends who've hit the lottery and has over six hundred thousand dollars in vehicles sitting in their yard, I think not. I ran the numbers on two of their license plates and both came back to the name of Eva Ramirez. She is the blonde headed woman you see in the picture, it was hard to find, but I found it. Franchesca Ramirez, she has one prior on her rap sheet and that was an attempted murder at the age of sixteen."

"Okay, well this definitely proves that he's involved with them. But which one of them do you think will be willing to come and testify on the stand at a jury trial to these accusations?" he asked with a straight face.

Thinking hard, she had to answer truthfully. "Probably neither, but it still doesn't fall short on our end."

Standing up she moved towards the door and looked out.

"Come in," she motioned with her hand.

Stepping out of the way, she allowed Justin to enter the room to take a seat.

"Can you remove your hat, please," Courtney asked, while standing behind him.

Huffing with anger, he removed the fitted cap exposing his face.

"Holy shit! Mr. Justin Rivers, I can't say that it's a pleasure to meet you, young man," McKenny said folding his arms.

"Now as I said, sir, he's going to be the key that help us put everything to an end."

"That's if I'm guaranteed my freedom to walk away from this shit. When you came and seen me in the Feds you didn't mention I would have to testify on my sister in front of a full fucking courtroom," Justin spat, cutting his eyes at Courtney.

"Well, what did you think was going to happen, Mr. Rivers? You've been mentioned in over ten unsolved cases from murder, drugs and even kidnapping. The list goes on, son. This is the way the law works," McKenny stated.

"Yeah, the way the law works, but what about me? If she finds out where I'm at, I'm fucking dead!"

"She won't find you, Justin. The DEA has the best witness protection program in the state of Georgia. It's our job to make sure you're safe," Courtney butted in.

"Right, just like your brother and father, right?"

"Excuse me?'

"You heard me. Your father was the crook of Smyrna and I wouldn't be in this bullshit if he wasn't beefing with my father over drug deals. The last time I saw you we were seventeen, a lot has changed in that small time. While you want to and further your career in being a super cop, your brother was killing everybody in the Marietta area because his father was too scared to arrest him. Now all this shit is back firing on y'all because you didn't stop the problem from the jump."

"That's a lie! Shaun has been arrested numerous times by the same force my father worked on."

"Yeah? For what? Assault, terroristic threats, possession of a firearm, right? He's never spent more than a month behind bars before he gets released to cause more havoc. Let me ask you something,

Camilla?" Justin said calling her by the codename she was given. "When's the last time you've heard from your brother?"

Sitting back in his seat, McKenny looked as if he was waiting for an answer also.

"What does that have to do with anything?" she countered.

"It has a lot to do with everything. Maybe you need to ask the people you're chasing on this big case. I'm sure they still have a piece of him laying around somewhere."

"You might want to watch your mouth before you talk yourself into another indictment, young man. Now you're not going to switch or flip anything to make this work how you want it. If you have information that's pertaining to anything that can help us, it'll be in your best interest to let us know, son," McKenny warned.

"If you can guarantee me I will do no prison time and you can get me out of the state, I'll help you take down everyone," Justin offered.

Looking at Courtney shake her head, he disregarded her action and shook Justin's hand.

"Deal."

***

Mozley Motel
Fulton Industrial Blvd.

"I don't think this is going to work, Stone. These bitches might tell on us, then what?" Reeses asked, stopping him before he entered the room.

"As long as you keep things on the low from Mariah, I think it'll work. We really have no other option, Rinesha. Or I can just start shooting people in the head in broad daylight and we can all catch a life sentence," Laylah said with a look as if she was serious.

"Baby, you gotta trust me. It'll work. If they don't agree, they won't walk out of this room," he ensured, unlocking the door.

As all three of them moved inside, Bang sat on the couch with his pistol in hand, fully awake. Not speaking as usual, he greeted Stone and the girls with a head nod and held his position.

Walking over to the two girls who were bound together in separate chairs. Reeses pulled the pillow cases from over their heads.

"Reeses! Bitch! I thought you and me were family. Why am I tied up eating McDonald's nuggets for the past week? You said you had a surprise for me and left a sister in this stinky hotel room," Sue shouted with a look of anger flushing through her red cheekbones.

"Sue, relax. There's a lot going on right now. I just need to make sure that my close ones are working with me instead of against me."

"Work against you? Bitch, have you lost your mind? I'm your ying, you're my yang. I'd never do you wrong. You pay me two hundred dollars to do your nails. Why would I mess up the way I pay my rent?" she replied, rolling her eyes as if Reeses violated a code.

"Sue, can you please just shut the hell up for about five minutes. I know you love me, okay," Reeses begged, as Stone stepped in front of Samantha.

"Look at me. I know you're probably terrified right now and I can understand why. But in order for you to make it out of this alive, you're gonna have to cooperate with us," he bargained with an intimidating stare.

"I swear I don't know where he is. I wouldn't lie to you. He doesn't even truly like me. He will never come no matter how many times I call," she panicked, speaking a thousand miles an hour. The large bags under her eyes were starting to turn black and guessing from the way her nose leaked, her body was craving from the devastating pain that corrupted her mind.

Things seemed to be going perfect for her a year ago before meeting Slick. His aggressive and possessive ways pulled her right back into the life that she'd desperately wanted to leave behind.

"Forget about Slick, he's not the problem on your hands right now. This is your son, correct?" Stone asked, pulling the small portrait from his pocket.

"Yes," she replied with a stressful expression.

"Do you love him?"

"Of course, I do. My son and mother are the only two people I have left. I have nothing else to live for but them."

"Well, the situation that's on the plate now will probably have you ready to commit suicide. Your son has been taken. Now before you start to spazz out and have a seizure it's up to you if he comes back dead or alive," Stone lied throwing the option up in the air.

"Please just tell me what I have to do," she pleaded, looking back and forth between all three of them.

He then cut the thick rope releasing the girl's hands and feet.

"Can anybody tell me where I play a part in this? Shit, I sat in a nasty room for a week. I wanna go on a dangerous mission, too," Sue voiced.

"Where did you find this bitch?" Laylah questioned.

Ignoring Sue's preposterous remark, she placed her attention on Bang and Stone.

"It's time."

***

For it to be a September night, the wind was cutting sharper than a knife and the moon had finally settled in the dark sky. Pulling his black Lincoln Continental in front of his home in Decatur, District Attorney Paul Edwards stepped out and strolled up his driveway. Placing the key in the door he entered his home and placed his briefcase on the floor.

"Honey, I'm home," he said out loud while making his way through the dark living room to find the light.

The sight of Stone sitting in his La-Z-Boy chair caused him to shiver in fear as he turned the switch.

"Who the fuck are you, man? Why are you in my home?' he stuttered after viewing the Beretta pistol resting in his lap.

"Mr. Edwards, please sit down. You're in no position to ask questions at this time."

"Where's my wife?' he questioned in a shaky tone.

"She's upstairs. There's someone with her. He's holding a gun to the center of her forehead with the hammer pulled back and if our conversation doesn't end well, she'll die and so will you."

Hearing Stone's words forced him to release a small amount of urine inside of his boxers. His heart felt as if it would burst at any minute and judging from the size of the big ass pistol, he knew the desired conversation was not about to end well.

"Sit down!" Stone repeated with more authority.

Taking a few steps back, he took a seat on the family couch. His feet were moving like a tap dancer and his hand rested in between his legs so he wouldn't completely piss on himself.

"Now I don't want to imply anything towards you, so I'll be very direct and I expect straight forward answers back."

No words came from the district attorney's mouth, he simply nodded.

"You've been playing with a very serious situation and that has officially created a full blown problem for a lot of people. Unfortunately, some aren't here to worry on the matter anymore. Lives have been given and sacrifices on many things have been forced away. All for one case that you refuse to rest easy on. Now you look like an honest man, you go to work to earn a living for you and your wife. I respect that. What I do is no different, I get up and make my way to the streets every day to feed the ones I love. But now that same family I feed is being torn apart because you can't respect the way we eat. Does Rinesha Rivers have bad blood with you or is it just something personal that you want to see her do a life sentence in prison?"

"I'm not in charge of the cases that I'm assigned to."

"I said straight answers, remember. Speak English!" Stone whispered aiming the pistol at his face.

Swallowing his spit, he released the rest of his urine inside of his pants.

"The DEA and FBI are all over the case. I'm not in a position to do anything about that matter."

"But you are the district attorney for the case which means you know everything down to the small details. Am I right?"

"Yes."

"Are there any surprise witnesses we should know about?"

"There's only two valid informants. Agent Courtney Myers and the defendant's brother Justin Rivers," he forced through trembling lips.

"I figured. I don't mean to impose on you in any way, but you're just a bull-headed state representative and your actions are forcing the hands of a lot of people. Now, is there a chance that you may happen to know where they're hiding her brother, do you?"

The lens of his glasses had begun to fog lightly from the warm sweat that ran down his forehead. Blinking his eyes numerous of times, he opened his mouth to reply.

"Don't lie!" Stone said, pulling the hammer back before he could spill any words.

"Mr. Rivers was being held in a hotel. The Days Inn off of Old National Highway, I was speaking to him yesterday after the State had him moved from the hospital on protection watch," he answered truthfully.

"I believe you," Stone agreed with a blank face.

Hearing the loud gunshot erupt upstairs, Edwards released a heap of shit in the lining of his boxers.

"Eliseee!" he screamed, breaking down in tears.

 Bang strolled down the steps with the weapon in his hand, then he walked towards the D.A. forcing him to place his palms around the handle.

"Now, this is the gun that you just murdered your wife with in cold blood, Mr. Edwards," Stone said, as Bang pushed away his sweaty hands and placed it inside a Ziploc bag.

"No," Edwards whined, as if he were in a bad dream.

"Yes, I'm afraid so, sir. Your selfish and egotistical ways have caused you to finally do the ultimate. You came home to find out that your wife was cheating on you according to these text messages that were sent to her secret lover an hour ago. Being that you were too much of a coward to step to the man, you came home and attacked your precious wife, who also has a black eye to prove this terrible crime."

"Oh, my god," he cried looking at the cell phone in Stone's hand.

"Looks like you only got one option to me, Mr. Edwards. You can dump her body, quit your job, and move out of the state. Or you can try to call the police after we leave and give them your side of the story that two men broke in and did it an hour before you came home. I don't know if that'll end well for you, but it's worth a try."

After observing Bang, wipe down most things that were touched. Stone stepped closer to the district attorney, grabbing his shoulder.

"We're hoping that we don't see you anytime soon. I'm gonna keep this little evidence close to me just in case someone tries to appear at Ms. Rivers' court date. I think we have an understanding, right?"

"Yes," he mumbled with an incoherent expression.

"Good, you have a good night, Mr. Edwards," Stone said, as he and Bang made their way out of the home.

***

Six Flags Drive

"Stepping through the door of the medium sized two bedroom safe house, Justin wrinkled up his nose as Courtney came in behind him securing the locks.

"I would have rather stayed at the hotel," he mumbled, heading into the living area.

"Well, unfortunately I don't have a choice but to follow protocol and that says to switch it up every two days on where we house you. You'll be fine for forty-eight hours," she said moving past him.

Staring at her round behind and healthy thighs, he licked his lips as she sat on the opposite couch across from him. Adjusting her holstered Glock 40 handgun, she removed her black backpack, sitting it on the glass table in front of her.

"The bathroom is down the hall on the right. And the guest room sits directly next to it. There are some things you can eat or cook in the kitchen," Courtney said before pulling out a paperback book and crossing her legs.

"What are you reading?" he asked trying to spark a conversation.

Rolling her eyes, she huffed before answering. "The Cuban Affair by Nelson Demille."

"What's that supposed to be like some drug empire shit?"

"No, it's more of a suspense novel, borderline mystery mixed with a few real life statistics."

"That shit sounds boring. I would've thought you'd like Urban or something like Romance."

"I've never been too tough on black novels."

"What? Urban is the best thing smoking. You ain't never read a Ca$h novel? Leo Sullivan? Nene Capri?"

"I've skimmed through a few. Over the years my mind has grown to like a variety of things besides my Black culture, I would say," she replied, bending two fingers for emphasis.

"Sitting in the Feds for ten years, you would grow to like Urban. It's more of relating to the things that brought you up, you know. Sometimes it's like I be right there in the book when they spilling those true poetic scenes of a Black person's life. Some books I read it kinda felt like they was telling my story. It takes you somewhere different, it's like you ain't even incarcerated no more," Justin said having a small flashback.

"I guess I wouldn't know," she said jumping back into her book.

"I still never got the chance to take you out on that date I asked for a while back."

"Justin, that was over eleven years ago and you must have forgot you had to leave for a while cause you wanted to be like the books you read in prison."

Chuckling, he nodded his head. "That was a low blow. It was never my intention to go to prison, Courtney. All of us didn't have a silver platter every night when we ate dinner, sweetheart."

Courtney sat her book on the table and crossed her arms. "Let's get something straight. If you're referring to my mother and father's money, you can flush that out of your head. Last time I checked I was shaking my ass next to your sister just to pay for college. No one gave me anything," she clarified with an angry expression.

"I mean just like you say, I guess I wouldn't know. You had a boyfriend that couldn't stop putting his hands on you. Then you disappeared to another state and return a full blown agent. Maybe if I would've got that one chance to be in your life we could've helped each other out with those differences, huh?"

"Maybe you need to take a nap to refresh your mind about a different subject," she shot back, picking up her book.

Smiling, he knew her buttons were being pushed.

"I don't mean to make you upset and I apologize if you feel disrespected in any way. I just want you to remember that you also have a past, Courtney. Nobody is perfect," he said with a sincere tone.

"As I told you before, I've never tried to be perfect. I chose to suffer with the sacrifices I've made to get to the position I'm in now. Regardless of how anyone sees me, I'm the only one who can judge that reflection in the mirror. Not you or anyone else."

"That's where you're wrong. Allah always has the last decision in things. Even when we make the choice for ourselves. In a certain light, I admire you for what you did. You actually found a path that you truly desired and you made it your reality. That's a beautiful thing to see. I might not be too happy with the whole agent in front of your name, but I accept it."

"We all have to learn how to let certain things take their course. You, Rinesha, even me. When that time comes, life will began to pour a lot smoother for us all."

Standing to his feet, Justin smirked. "For some reason, I have a hard time accepting that from you."

"Why? It's the truth," she stated.

"I never said it wasn't. I just think you have a problem following your own theory. I remember a time when you had your course set."

"Really? And when was that?"

"Eleven years ago when you said you loved me," he replied, walking off towards the guest room.

As Courtney sat there fighting off his words with silence Justin turned around and   stared at her gorgeous red face.

"Good night," he mumbled before disappearing through the dark hallway.

Chris Green

Chapter 14

Gwinnett County 7:30 am

After dialing Stone's number, Torez placed the phone to his ear while waiting patiently for an answer.

"Who's this?"

"Mr. Stone?"

"I said, who is this?"

"I presume that I am speaking with the right person, since you continue to repeat the same shit anyway!" Torez spoke in more of an aggravated tone.

"That all depends on who's on the other end of my fucking line."

Sliding a hand through his medium length goatee, Torez smiled before standing to his feet.

"The name is Torez."

"Alright, Torez, what can I do for you?" Stone questioned.

"You can tell me what the fuck happened to my son, mother-fucker."

"I'm afraid I don't know what the hell you're talking about. Now maybe you were looking for a number down to Mexico or Brazil cause I think you called the wrong person," Stone replied through the phone in a smooth voice.

"Not according to your brother, Shakur, my friend. A couple of nights ago my son Hector was killed in this punta's auntie's home. It's amazing to me that you say you don't know, when he says you're the one who pulled the trigger. Now I'll be very brief because me don't do a lot of back and forth. We can meet to discuss this problem like grown men because quite frankly, I'm ready to kill everyone associated with him and you."

"First of all, you've been lied to. Shakur is trying to do whatever he can to get away from the large ticket that has been placed on his head. Everyone and their mother is out looking for him to put a bullet in between his eyes. Now I'm kind of positive on how all this took place. Feel free to stop me if you hear something incorrect. He came to you pleading for mercy because you heard that he was behind your son's death. Being that you listened it gave him the opportunity for him to throw the blame on someone he happens to be running from. I'm sorry to say it, Torez, but you've been tricked," Stone stated with a convincing story.

"Is that so? And what is the price for him?"

"Eight hundred grand, but if you're speaking in our language, twenty uncut keys of heroin."

Hearing the extreme numbers made Torez' palm itch instantly. A man of his caliber didn't get to a certain degree from being stupid and if someone was willing to place eighty percent of a million in dope on your head, the reason had to be critical.

"How can I be sure that this bounty is authentic?" Torez asked, ready to throw Shakur under the bus for the healthy payday.

"Easy, you can go and shoot the man in the head for murdering your son and kill a problem for me also, and I can keep my product. Or you can bring the son of a bitch to me, receive your dope and watch me execute the man who took your seed in front of you. It's your choice." Stone gave the option, waiting on an answer.

"When I'm ready I'll give the call, homes," he responded before hanging up.

Stone placed the phone back in his pocket and inhaled deeply. He knew for a fact that mind games were easy when it came to simple people. The small word was spreading around that Torez was lurking for him because of the death of his son. Knowing that Shakur would pull a coward move he was already two steps ahead of the game. There was nothing like a little paperwork to bribe most people into doing anything. A man would be willing to break his neck or even tell on his mother to receive twenty kilos of pure dog food.

Crossing another task off his list, he prepared himself for the next. Finding Justin to show him that disloyalty was unforgivable.

***

Overlook Atlanta

"Yo, Slick?" Tremaine called out, making his way through the apartment door.

The untidy living room caused him to stop in his tracks.

"Bro, what the fuck do you got going on?" he questioned as Slick rounded the hallway corner.

Tremaine was an old associate, who would practically be down for whatever cause until Slick got the big head leaving him behind in the hood to hustle crumbs. Even though he was fumed about how he was treated, he never forgot, but forgave for the sake of being a good nigga. After seeing Slick moving slyly around the hood for the past few days, he couldn't help but link up.

"Shh! Come in and lock the door. Did anybody follow you?" he asked with a paranoid look on his face.

"Nigga, you tripping. I told you I would be back in thirty minutes after I ran to the store and got the shit you ask me for. What the hell happened to the living room? It look like a tornado flew through this motherfucker," he replied, locking the door.

"I know my mind ain't playing tricks on me, my nigga. I keep hearing this fucking clicking sound every five minutes. It's like it's gets louder and louder and I still can't find it. I tore this bitch up and still don't know how I'm moving past it," Slick said with a serious expression.

Listening for a few seconds, silence loomed through the air causing Tremaine to look at him awkwardly.

"Are you alright, bro? You not acting like yourself."

"Hell nah, I'm not aite! That bitch is trying to get me killed, I know it."

"Who are you talking about?" he asked, turning a chair over to its right side so he could take a seat.

"You know who!"

"No, the fuck I don't, bro. That's why I'm asking. You ain't said nothing to me about nobody trying to get you spilled, bruh," Tremaine stated while lighting a Newport.

Looking around clueless, he stepped closer before speaking as if someone was eavesdropping.

"Reesess."

Staring with a raised eyebrow, Tremaine burst into a fit of laughter and pulled an ounce of marijuana out of his pocket.

"Nigga, you done lost your rabid ass mind. You think your niece is trying to whack you? Bruh, what the fuck have you been smoking?"

"Laugh that shit up, nigga. I ain't motherfucking crazy. That bitch put a hit on my head for all types of money. Everywhere I motherfucking go nigga's busting at me and shit. I can't trust nobody. I think she the reason I keep hearing these voices," he stressed with animosity flowing through his veins.

Sitting down his blunt, Tremaine could see the trouble in his eyes. It was unlike Slick, a true gangsta by nature to fear anything or anyone. But the story he was hearing just didn't add up.

"Why in the fuck would little Rinesha want you dead?"

"That's what the fuck I want to know. Word going around that I had something to do with her mom and bitch ass daddy coming up dead. If I did that shit I'd be man enough to motherfucking say it," he lied, reaching for the cigarette in Tremaine's hand.

Pulling on the nicotine like his life depended on it, Tremaine continued to twist up the weed.

"I ain't even gone lie, Slick, a lot of shit was going around saying that you got rid of Jimmie about some paper. You know I don't believe that mess, but you know how the streets spread rumors, bro. You can't let that shit get to you."

"How could you kill your own mother?"

Slick heard the creaky voice whisper lightly in his ear. Jumping as if he was struck with a bullet, he pulled his pistol, ready to fire.

"I know you heard that!" he yelled, looking at Tremaine.

Raising his hands slowly, he leaned back in the chair.

"Bro! Put the gun down. You spazzing right now. You my dog, but I think you need some help. Just let me call somebody to take you down to the hospital."

"If you thinking about picking up a phone, I will blow yo shit across the room. Get up and get the fuck out. Now!" he demanded.

Rising out the seat, Tremaine dropped the blunt from his mouth and backed up until he reached the front door. Opening it up, he stepped out, closing it lightly behind him.

Locking it, Slick posted against the door frame with his eyes roaming back and forth. His heart almost came to a halt after hearing the annoying clicking sounds run through his eardrum. Covering them with his hands, Jimmie's voice spoke directly to him loud and clear.

"I thought I was your brother!"

The spooky tone sent him over the edge, making his gun erupt out of fear.

Boc! Boc! Boc! Boc! Boc!

Running towards the bathroom he tripped hitting the floor and quickly stumbled back to his feet. Getting inside he slammed the door nearly knocking the hinges loose.

The torment of his dirty deeds were starting to kick in harder than ever. All he could envision was the bloody faces of murdered family members haunting him every second. He knew that it was only a sign that his time was coming. His mind was already made up. Before he died by Reesess' hand, he would take his own soul instead of giving her the satisfaction of seeing him lose this treacherous game.

***

Two days later
Lincoln Cemetery

Sitting in front of Salim's closed casket, Stone couldn't help but shed a few tears for his fallen Muslim brother. It had been a journey for them both, but his vow was to always protect the younger Ahks from all harm. Spending time in prison with them all, he learned and understood life better. There was a difference between the ones who stood by you and the ones who genuinely loved you from the heart. Money, protection and numerous other miscellaneous things could get most men to stand by your side and have not an ounce of respect or love for you. Moving through the struggles together with nothing, built a bond and brotherhood that would last forever.

Reciting the funeral prayer and offering Dua for the brother, his cell rang after he stood to his feet. Observing the unknown digits, he answered.

"Speak."

"Mr. Stone, I figured that we can resolve this issue today. We can meet at a place of your choice," Torez spoke through the receiver.

"I'll text you the address in five minutes," he replied, ending the call.

It was amazing how the power of Allah worked when pain was troubling one of his children. He always found a way to ease it.

Making it back to the car, he got in and looked over at Reeses and Laylah.

"I found Shakur," he said, before cranking the car and pulling off.

***

Sitting behind the abandoned elementary school, Stone and the girls waited patiently to see if Torez would show up.

"How do we know that these Mexicans aren't trying to ambush us? We're sitting here with twenty kilos of heroin and we don't even know if they have Shakur for sure," Reeses said making sense.

"Because Mexicans are thirsty when it comes to money, baby. They won't fuck up any chance they have to get a come up. Especially when you're talking about dope," Stone clarified with surety.

"He's definitely right. Most of the Mexicans me and Mariah have dealt with are straight un-cut business. If it has anything to do with money their attention locks in like a child on candy."

"Speaking of the devil," Stone said watching the two Durango trucks pull inside the parking lot.

"Maybe we should see what they do first," Reeses said, a little paranoid.

"Fuck that. We're getting out. If anyone of them makes the wrong move they'll die before they can blink twice," Laylah stated calmly.

Trusting her cousin's judgment Stone grabbed the large duffel off the floor as all three of them stepped out of the car, guns in hand.

As the Durango's came to a halt, Torez and four armed Mexicans stepped out with Shakur directly behind them.

Looking back at Shakur, Torez motioned for him to step forward.

"This is the man that you say killed my son, correct?" he asked in a displeased manner.

"Yes, that's him," Shakur mouthed, looking over at Stone.

Stepping forward, Torez shook his head. "Do you have what we agreed on?"

Hearing the question caused Shakur's stomach to plunge in fear as he stared at Torez with a confused face.

Opening the bag, Stone dug inside pulling out one of the raw squares and tossed it over. Watching one of the goons pick it up, he began to examine it. Sticking a knife through the tough plastic, he looked at Torez, nodding his head.

Smiling, his henchmen picked up the duffel as he walked away.

"Wait, what's going on?" Shakur asked, watching the men load up to leave.

"You say that's the man that murdered my son. Turns out he feels a different way, homes. Seems like a personal matter to me, my friend," Torez said, leaving him in the middle of the lot as he climbed back in his vehicle and pulled away.

Standing less than five feet away from Laylah, Stone and Reeses, Shakur was stuck with a disoriented facial expression. Walking over to him, Reeses spat directly into his face.

"There's no point in me wasting too many words, so I'll be brief. Enjoy hell," she smiled evilly, before making her way back to the car.

Seeing Laylah and Stone step forward, he held his breath.

"You won't make it into paradise if you kill me, Stone. I'm still Muslim," he barked, knowing his time was near.

"Alhamdulilah," Stone replied before he and Laylah released an excessive amount of bullets into his body.

Making their way quickly back to the car, Laylah smiled after getting in.

"Being around you two will bring a very bad side out of me."

Chapter 14

10:00pm
Days Inn Hotel

Smiling with a devilish grin, Justin slammed down the ten of diamonds.

"That's a fucking casino, girl. You ain't got not one motherfucking point," he laughed, looking at her small bundle of cards.

"It's because you're cheating, nigga. I know for a fact I had the deuce of spade," she lied, flipping through her hand.

"Courtney, you thinking about the deuce of clubs. That's four games, one more before I glove that ass."

Standing up she tossed the cards in his face. "That's definitely not about to happen!"

The small black shorts she wore hugged her apple with a perfect snug showing off her smooth juicy legs. Her curly hair hung freely making her freckles even more attractive. Justin couldn't help but stare at the amazing beauty that stood before him.

"What? Why are you staring at me?" she asked, standing back on her legs like a stallion.

"You're even more beautiful now then you were when we was younger."

Mmmhmm, sometimes I think back and wish I would've never fell for those little lines from you. I'd probably still have my virginity."

Standing up he stood face to face with her. He was so close, her Paris Hilton perfume started to crawl up his nose.

"Are you okay?" Courtney questioned, staring him up and down as if he were violating.

Instead of replying with words, Justin wrapped his hand around the back of her neck and slid his tongue into her mouth for a passionate kiss. Feeling her kitty tingle, she closed her eyes and pushed lightly away from his grasp.

"Please don't do that, Justin. I still have a job to do," she uttered while trying to stop her heart from beating furiously.

"Says who? I can't deny the fact that I still hold the same love for you from when I was seventeen. You were the last woman I was with, Courtney. It's hard not to want you," he said, caressing the side of her face.

"A lot of things have changed, Justin. You can't just expect everything to still be the same."

Controlling the strong urge to pull her into the bedroom, he nodded his head understanding her reasoning.

"I'm sorry. You're right. I'm just gonna go downstairs and grab me a soda from the vending machine. You want anything?"

Giving him a stern look, he laughed.

"What I do now?"

"You know you can't be leaving out of the room, Justin. If you get in trouble or leave, it'll be on me."

"Girl, I'm not about to go nowhere. I'm going down here to get something to drink and coming right back."

"I'm not playing with you, Justin. By the time I finish using the restroom you better be back in here," she said, with a serious tone before walking off.

Opening the room door he stepped out, shaking his head. It was so difficult to be in the same room with a woman you shared so much chemistry with and couldn't do anything. Even though he knew Courtney still possessed the same love, he respected her position.

Getting down to the bottom of the breezeway, he stepped in front of the Coca-Cola machine and zipped his jacket from the wind that hung in the air.

"As-salamu-laikum."

Jumping slightly, he turned his head. Staring at Stone, who stood a few feet away from him, gun in hand.

"Wa-laikum-as-salam," he replied knowing that he was caught down bad.

"Looks like you feeling better, Ahkie. Any reason why you just left from the hospital without letting us know anything?" Stone asked taking a few steps forward.

"I got a lot of shit going on that I need to handle on my own, bro. It's nothing personal."

"I think it is personal when you thinking about testifying against Reeses. That's clearly something that should be mentioned to the brothers. Don't you think? Not just that. You were planning on taking all of us down with you. Everyone came together to assist you with a problem and we were being played the entire time."

"I was never gonna go through with it, bro"

"Bullshit. We seen the paperwork, Ahk. Salim is dead right now because of you, nigga."

"What?" Justin mumbled, feeling his heart drop from the statement.

"Don't look surprised now. What the fuck would make you turn state on the same ones who love your dumb ass?"

"You don't know the shit I had to go through just to make it back home to my sister. If I wouldn't have agreed with what they asked me, she would probably be dead right now. They came to me with a new indictment and the plea was a life sentence. When they asked me to help them build a case on Reeses, I told them to kiss my ass. Word got back to me from the streets that she was kidnapped. Working with them was the only chance I had to see daylight on saving her life, bro. I had no choice," Justin stated truthfully.

"You could've called on me. You could've warned us before any of this went down, Justin. But you didn't," Stone replied pulling the hammer back on his gun.

Stepping around the corner smoothly, Courtney leveled her pistol with two hands.

"Put it down, Stone and I'm not going to ask you twice," she said with authority in her tone.

Cutting his eyes at her, he looked back at Justin and aimed for his head.

Boom!

Her Glock 40 erupted viciously in the small hallway sending a slug through his arm. Watching his weapon fall, she quickly picked it up.

"Justin, go and grab everything from the room and get the car, now," she yelled, keeping her aim on Stone.

Leaning on the wall, he held his arm as Justin moved quickly past him. The crimson blood that began to soak his sleeve caused him to breathe harder.

"You've mixed yourself into something that you're not gonna be able to step away from," he said through clenched teeth.

"Or you're gonna end up getting yourself killed trying to do something that I refuse to let happen. I understand that Rinesha is mad, but you can't change something that's already been done."

"That's where you're wrong. He's not going to make it through that trial. Neither one of you will. You might as well put a bullet in between my eyes now, because the job will be finished," Stone threatened with a smirk that sent chills through her body.

"Courtney, let's go!" Justin said now fully dressed. "Just leave him, please."

Backing out of the breezeway, they made their way to the unmarked Impala and skated quickly out of the parking lot.

***

Downtown Atlanta
1:15am

"Even if his story is true, that bitch shot me," Stone said as Laylah finished patching up his arm.

"And that's something you should've expected from an Agent. She could've killed you," Laylah said with a sarcastic smirk.

Reeses sat quietly on the bed pondering on the information Stone delivered to her. the new cold-hearted side of her said wash every sob excuse out of her head and have him executed on the spot for his betrayal. But the family side of her pleaded that he was actually telling the truth. Within the past year all of their siblings and close friends had been dropping like flies. Justin was literally the last piece of blood she had left besides the cousins she recently discovered.

"Don't dwell on it too long, Rinesha. It's kind of obvious he was scared to tell you exactly what was going on. I would be nervous too if it had anything to do with building a Federal case on my sister," Laylah said.

"So, does that make it right? Excuses are only for people who accept them. It's just certain things that you can never take back," Stone said sliding a shirt over his head.

"No one ever said it was right, but if you want to be technical, he hasn't snitched or testified on her. The statements only showed that he agreed to do it. To be honest the only way you would know what's he gonna do is if we wait for the trial."

"And that could easily be too late for us all," he replied walking out to the balcony.

"At the end of the day I stand behind you, no matter what decision you make. That's what family is for," Laylah smiled.

Nodding and blowing her a small kiss, Reeses already had her mind made up.

Chris Green

Chapter 16

Kennesaw, Ga.
7:30am

Stepping out of the house, Knox made his way to the parked BMW M760 and got inside. Pulling the red Kush from his pocket, he grabbed a Backwood rolled up and quickly filled it with marijuana. The sun had just begun to rise high and his morning wake up was past due. Lighting the large spliff, his eyes roamed around the enormous driveway. It wasn't like the guards to leave any part of the home unsecured. It aroused a slight suspicion, but the good aura of the weed instantly dismissed it.

Cranking the car, he finished off the last piece of his joint and glanced down at the small sticky note attached to the radio. The white clouds caused him to squint his eyes to read the words.

"Time will turn family into enemies and enemies will take their time to see family fail."

"Superstition," he mumbled in his thick island voice.

Before he could place the blunt back into his mouth, the car exploded, killing him instantly.

***

Laying sound asleep in her large bed, Mariah squirmed under the covers from the cool breeze that was flowing through her room.

Boommm!

The ground shaking explosion caused her to jump up from the bed and grab her pistol out of the nearby nightstand. Mariah tried to stop her heart from racing, as she took tiny steps to her bedroom door. Another explosive erupted right under her feet. Her mind went into overdrive wondering where Knox was. Hearing gunshots explode, sent Mariah from fear to full blown panic mode. Now she knew that whatever was taking place at that time was nothing to be relaxed about.

As Mariah cracked her bedroom door, a billow of smoke lingered throughout the hallway. Aiming her 9mm handgun she stepped out of the room. Using her forearm, she covered half of her face as she walked towards the staircase that led downstairs. Her cold feet were now shivering and it felt as if she was walking on eggshells. The nervousness was starting to kick in and the silence was making it more uncomfortable.

Coughing from the thick black smoke, Mariah walked slowly down to the bottom floor.

"Hi, big sister," Frost whispered, startling her.

Turning around, Mariah aimed the gun, but received a fist directly to her nose. Grabbing her wrist, Frost twisted with a hard grip, breaking it instantly.

"Agghhh!" Mariah cried out in pain as her gun fell to the floor.

Sliding back with her feet, Mariah stared into her sister's eyes.

"You're not related to me! You were a mistake and that's the reason you're angry, Frost!" She spat.

Looking at the three armed men who stood behind her she knew the fate of her guards wouldn't end well. Since she knew about the vicious and wicked morals of Frost's character, it was a guarantee that she was next.

"That's where you're wrong, love. I'm not angry, I'm just frustrated. Chasing you stupid cunts around has literally drained me dry. I've spent years waiting for the day I could meet my flesh and blood. Now it seems that you're not happy to see me," she smiled, bending down.

"If you think you've gone unnoticed, you're in for a surprise. Everyone knows you're sliding around and it's only a matter of time before you're buried and mailed in a box back to where you came from," Mariah panted, catching her breath.

Laughing, Frost looked around at her stale faced guards as if she'd just heard the best joke of her life.

"You're so silly. I've never tried to hide from you or your pathetic little family. To be honest I thought that you all would have taken the warning signs and stayed under the radar. I guess we all make a small mistake here and there, huh?" she asked, rolling her eyes and smirking. The sarcasm was obvious.

"Just go ahead and kill me! You still won't win!" Mariah smirked with blood dripping from her nose.

"Oh no, sister, it's not that easy. See I came for three but I only have one. Where are the other two?"

"You'll never get me to tell you anything about my family."

Sucking her teeth, Frost shook her head in a disappointed manner. "They'll actually come looking for you and when they do, I'll be waiting and torture them the same way."

On cue, one of her deadly henchmen slammed a hard foot across Mariah's face, knocking her unconscious. Picking up her limp body, they headed through the destroyed front door.

"Call Eva and tell her to let my mother know that we are on the way," she said looking back at one of the men.

"Yes ma'am."

***

"So, that solves the problem with Justin, even though I don't agree. That still leaves the problem with the cop. I guess she's not going to testify either?" Stone asked with sarcasm pouring through his tone.

His mind still couldn't process how Reeses decided to let Justin be and wait until the trial to see what move he would make. It was like playing Russian Roulette with the joker himself. A gambling game was meant to play only if you were winning and Stone felt that she was walking into a trap where she was bound to lose.

"That's where I come in, leave her to me. All I need is Mariah's approval and she'll be dead within the next four hours," Laylah stated with confidence.

Staring with a blank face, Reeses tapped them both and pointed towards their large home that was engulfed with black smoke.

"What the hell?" Stone mumbled, pulling in the parking lot past the smoking BMW.

"Oh my god, Mariah!" Laylah screamed in a panic, before jumping out the car with her gun in hand.

Seeing her cousin run into the home, Reeses and Stone stepped out directly behind her. The catastrophe their eyes were witnessing was like something they'd never seen before. The bodies of her guards were scattered on the side of the home. The vehicle in front of them was roasting as if it were sitting over an open grill and the front door of the house was replaced with a hole big enough to drive a medium sized U-Haul through.

Making their way inside slowly, Laylah was moving back down the steps.

"She's not here," she said on the verge of tears.

"What the fuck is going on? What do you mean she's not here? Where else can she be?" Reeses asked with her hands running through her hair.

"I don't know! Here phone was in the room, this is not good," she replied, dialing a set of numbers into her cell.

Listening to her mother answer, she spoke very quickly. "Mom, something is very wrong. I came home to the house destroyed and I can't find Mariah."

"What do you mean you can't find her?" Tiffany asked in an extremely serious tone,

"She's gone, Mommy, I don't know what to do," she replied spilling a load of tears down her cheeks.

"Laylah! Listen to me. Go and find her, I don't care if you have to kill the entire city. Get her back. Now!"

"But, Mom, Dad told me"

"Laylah, stop it! Your father is dead. I'm giving you permission. Go and get your sister."

"Yes ma'am," she said before hanging up.

"Laylah, what are we going to do?" Reeses asked watching her walk off towards the car garage.

Following her steps in silence, they watched her remove a false wall exposing an arsenal of weapons. Pulling down a double shoulder holster, she snapped it around her body. Grabbing the two black Rutger 9mm handguns, she placed them inside the cuffs of her arm and began to load the rest in a small bag.

"Hey! What are you thinking about doing?" Stone asked, sensing her energy.

Looking him in the eyes, her face told it all. "What I always do. Fix the problem," she replied with a staid expression.

"Then we are coming with you!" he stated, grabbing Reeses hand while he clutched on his pistol tighter.

Nodding, she made her way back to the car with both of them standing firmly behind her with whatever action she took. Only a few knew of Laylah's excessive and extreme degree for harming others when the order was given. Getting the permission from Tiffany was a green light to eliminate whatever stepped in her path of finding Mariah.

Chris Green

Chapter 17

Six Flags Drive

After stepping out of the hot, steamy shower, Courtney threw on her large sleeping tee shirt and wrapped her hair into a bun. After applying lotion to her legs and arms, she made her way out of the bathroom. Heading back to the guest room she was sleeping in, she paused in front of Justin's door. His back was turned to her as he stared out of the window, while sitting down in a desk chair. His head hung low and judging from his posture she could tell something was wrong.

Knocking lightly on the door frame, she took a few steps inside. "Are you okay?"

Ignoring her, he kept his attention on the sun that was beaming directly on his face. Moving closer to him is when she spotted the stream of tears coming down his chin.

"I sit and ask myself sometimes is it truly meant for me to even be on this earth," he spoke, biting his bottom lip. "I've caused so much pain. I've failed at nearly everything there was besides making my way to a prison cell. It's like I'm not even alive, ya know."

Listening to his words, she sat in silence as he continued to pour out his feelings.

"Sitting in the Feds, I called home to hear my father was murdered before I could even be booked inside the county jail. Not too long after that, my mother died from a fucking heroin overdose. My little sister was left to be raised by a slut stripper, who would place her mouth on any nigga that'll toss a dollar in her face. It's been ten long ass years and I'm back in the same spot," he mumbled with a lifetime of pain in his words

Using her hand, she wiped the tears off his face.

"Beating yourself up about a situation that's already done is only a backtrack. You've become the man you are because you had no choice. It's the way that Allah created you. Some days I ponder on decisions I could have made. If only I took the chance to think before acting, a lot of things could have been so much better for me."

"You've become a beautiful and intelligent woman because you chose to, Courtney. No one can be mad or fault you for the decisions you picked. You turned out to be everything that I knew you could," he said with a sincere look.

"No one can be mad, but I still fault myself. Sometimes I feel if I would've gave you a better chance, I could have saved you. You were a great person and I knew your intentions for me were wonderful. There were things I wanted to tell you, but I couldn't. I felt I let you down. A few months after you took my virginity, I found out I was pregnant."

Lowering his head, he rubbed a hand across his face.

"You were already in the process of being sentenced and I was so scared, Justin. I didn't know what else to do," she admitted while holding his hand.

Justin glanced out the window for a few seconds before he turned his attention back to her. Placing a small peck on her fingertips, he smiled.

"I still love you, always will."

Feeling the love flowing from his words, she leaned in, kissing his lips softly. As their tongues danced and twirled with a heated passion, Courtney could feel her pussy lips throbbing under the shirt she wore.

Her emotions were running high and it had been forever since she was pleased with any type of sexual satisfaction. His firm lips took her breath away and the tingling sensation between her legs couldn't contain the fire that was craving to blaze up.

Pulling the shirt over her head, she stood before him looking more amazing than a swimsuit model. Her legs were smooth with a small patch of hair covering her vagina. Her six pack blended perfectly with her B-cup breast. Her nipples were light brown and her round booty sat up perfectly on her back as if she'd been doing squats for five years straight. Justin's manhood stood up with a stiff movement trying to bulge out of his pants as she began to undo his zipper. Releasing him from his boxers, Courtney stared at his masterpiece and wasted no time climbing on top of him. Wrapping his hands around her round behind, he rotated his rod in a circle on her sweet lips until she slid down on his length.

"Oh God!" she moaned, as she filled her tight tunnel.

Sliding her hands down to his neck, Courtney leaned forward gliding gently on his rod. Giving her a small nibble on the neck, Justin's finger trailed down the crack of her ass until he penetrated the spot. Courtney moaned in pleasure. Her body was turning hot from his delicate touch. Pushing in deeper. She gasped as her pussy pulsated in satisfaction. As he latched down onto Courtney's nipple, he sucked on it roughly like a newborn baby. Justin's pace sped up feeling the juices of her kitty flow down his leg.

"Fuck," she whispered as her eyes rolled to the back of her head. Putting his hands on the chair, her plump behind bounced smoothly matching his rhythm.

"I never stopped loving you,' he admitted, whispering in her ear.

"Tell me how much you love me," she commanded, riding harder. Her ass began to clap loudly against his legs. Within two minutes she was busting her first orgasm on top of him.

Justin stood to his feet and carried her over to the bed. Easing her down, he turned her on all fours, re-entering her. Courtney flinched while looking back at him laying his sex game down. The euphoria her body was in hypnotized her mind as she tried to keep up with his addictive stroke.

Justin's hands slid down the side of Courtney's thighs and back up to her hips. Gripping them he began to feed her womanhood the dick until she oozed a thick creamy orgasm on his member. Feeling the pressure build up inside of him, he pulled out releasing his semen over her plump backside.

"We can just leave, Courtney. We can walk away together," Justin offered pulling her down beside him.

Exhaling deeply, Courtney rubbed his cheek, as she mustered up a warm smile. "I wish it was that easy, Justin."

"It is. All we have to do is just go. Courtney, Reeses is rich, and I'm not talking about two, three million. We would be straight, forever."

"Your sister is trying to have you murdered right now. Or did you forget about that."

"I know my baby sister. It's more likely that Stone is pushing the issue instead of her. She's only mad because she thinks I'm going to testify against her at trial. I'll rather die before I do some shit like that to her," he clarified, looking into Courtney's eyes.

"I don't know, Justin. The DEA wouldn't be too happy about me pulling a stunt like that. It's possible they can arrest me," she stated with a serious gaze.

"They can't arrest you if you quit, baby."

"I just really need time to think about a lot of things. Please," she said, kissing his lips.

"Say less," he mouthed dropping the subject.

She could tell from his tone that her answer was one that he didn't want to hear. Everything she worked for her entire life would be on the line if she pulled a move on what he was asking. Intertwining her heart with a criminal family was something that was bound to end terribly wrong. Her mind warned her that it wasn't a chance worth taking.

***

Mariah opened her eyes as the nauseating feeling took over body. She puked so violently that her clothes were completely covered, as she trembled uncontrollably. The large room she was sitting in housed nothing but a bed and a few pictures that were lined on the wall. Her ankles and hands sported a pair of shiny handcuffs and her body was posted in a chair wrapped with bundles of strong sisal fiber. Moving her neck, she instantly felt pain from the hard kick that was delivered to her face. Her jaw was slightly swollen and the twine that was laced around her body cut into her every time she moved.

She watched anxiously as the door slowly opened. A guard stepped in with a wicked smile. His dark glasses hid his eyes as he walked slowly towards her.

"Aren't you a little cutie," he said flashing his crooked teeth, while sliding two fingers through her brown hair.

Mariah shot a glob of spit in his face. The fluid ran down the bridge of his nose, which made him furious in a matter of seconds. Cocking his fist back, he stopped after hearing Frost speak.

"If you touch her, I'll blow your brains out and feed it to the dogs," she said with her gun in hand. "Now get the fuck out."

"Yes ma'am," he replied.

Straightening his suit, he made his way out of the door, closing it behind him.

"He can get out of hand sometimes, don't mind him. On the other hand, I came to have a little fun with my sister," Frost stated showing Mariah the bottle of rubbing alcohol.

Frost put her pistol on the edge of the bed and stepped in front of Mariah.

"You know what amazes me? Not once have any one of you offered an apology or even a little empathy for my situation. Instead you continued to make a recursive move. No one wanted to rectify or sit down and talk as a family. You dissed me as if I were a prostitute or a junkie begging for change and I still turned out magnificent."

"You want to reconcile differences, but this is reality, Frost. This family doesn't forgive nor do we forget. You blame everyone else for the way things have turned out, but do you see what you're doing now? You're in denial and you truly don't care about making anything better. It's just about you winning, that's all. You felt like you lost your entire life and you just want to win," Mariah replied at a low tone.

Balling up her face, Frost pulled a sharp razor from her pocket, slicing Mariah across the leg. Opening the alcohol, she splashed it twice over the fresh cut making Miriah scream dreadfully.

"Winning, huh!" Frost yelled making a cut on the opposite leg.

"Aghhh!" Mariah howled in pain as she shook uncontrollably trying to get free.

The thin twine was starting to bite at her skin, splitting it slowly with every movement she made.

"I graduated from the best schools, exceeded limits at the best college. I've had whatever I wanted on this earth since I popped out the pussy. I even attended marksman training just to top whatever challenge presented itself. I've won at everything imaginable, bitch. I want revenge!" Frost raged, swiping the razor across Mariah's right cheek. Frost squeezed the entire bottle of alcohol in her face. She prepared to jam the blade into Mariah's throat.

"Frost, that's enough!" her mother stated walking into the room.

Turning around to face her, she gritted her teeth.

"I said that's enough! She's still your sister. Leave until you calm down," she spoke in a soft voice as if she were seventy years old.

Frost dropped the razor on the floor, she snatched her pistol off the bed and stormed out, slamming the door behind her.

Breathing harshly from the assault, Mariah watched as the woman dragged a chair from the corner and placed it in front of her. Mariah stared into her cold eyes as she watched her take a seat. Her blonde hair laid straight down her back and her pale skin glowed with a glossy hue as if she'd bathed in a tub of baby oil. Judging from her curvy hips and thick thighs, she couldn't have been older than forty. The only creepy thing that stuck out was her right eye, that was partially closed like it was glued together.

"You've grown into a beautiful woman. I remember when you were no more than two years old," she said lighting the Newport short that was between her fingers.

Staring at her with hatred, Mariah knew that the woman must have been another crazy ass female related to the stupid misborn who'd recently walked out of the room. Her face definitely wasn't familiar and she wasn't going to remember a memory from the age of two for sure. Her energy was physically drained and evaluating the situation in her head she was bound to die in the exact spot she sat unless Laylah magically got a hint on where to find her.

"Your name's Mariah, correct?" she asked dragging on her cigarette.

"Who are you?" she replied with of disgust. "Just tell her to kill me and get it over with. You don't have to stall me out for information because I'm not going to say anything," Mariah said through clenched lips as her cuts started to burn.

Pulling a napkin from her pocket, she wiped the blood gently away from the wound on her face.

"My name is Coco," she replied, doing the same thing to the splits on her leg.

Mariah's thoughts were starting to run wild. She didn't know why the lady in front of her was being so nice after frost just tried to torture her. Catching the resemblance she realized that the woman had to be her mother.

"I know that Frost can go overboard sometimes. But that's just the way she was raised. Of course it was never meant for her to use it against her own family. I guess it just grew on her naturally. None of this was meant to happen, but I can't help the way that she feels," Coco stated pulling on the Newport again.

"Oh really? You sit in front of me with an excuse as if you're here to save me. I'm gonna fill you in on something. I'm nineteen years old, I'm not from a fucking country town where they milk cows in order to eat cereal for breakfast. I'm very intelligent, I've been in control of my family's business for three long years. Not because I'm the first born, because I was smart enough to hold the position. In order to hold a position it takes courage that takes mental and moral strength. It implies firmness of the mind for one to hold their own against the opposition or even close ones. It eventually builds an implication of stubbornness, persistence and the unwillingness to accept defeat. You raised your daughter to be a killer, you forced her to see that there is no other way she can lose. To never show any physical weakness."

Looking at her with surprise, Coco knew that she was spilling the truth.

"How do I know these things? Because I have the strictest parents at home, who've just so happened to instruct me to be the same way. No disrespect but you don't have to lie in order for me to respect what you're doing, because if the ball was in my court, all would be mutual," Mariah said with a small nod.

Bobbing her head gently, Coco smirked while discarding her cigarette butt on the floor.

"You're very witty for your age, sweetheart and I respect your choice of words. Unfortunately, I've never been a decisive person. I've sat around most of my life accepting things the way they came. I never asked for much. I stripped and even sold my body sometimes just to make sure I could make a living for me and my sister. Trust me, selling ass was very hard to accept, but I did whatever was necessary to make a way. One day things actually started to look a little brighter for me. I was offered a golden opportunity to show mother fuckers just how much of a bad bitch I was. To shine like a star out in Beverly Hills. That's when I met the person that ruined my life forever. Your father," she said staring into space as if she was having to relive that moment.

"So, you had a child with a murderer. A man who was at the peak of his criminal life and truly didn't have any intentions on settling. You laid down and opened your legs knowing that there was a possibility that he would abandon you. Not to mention that he already had two women with children fighting for his love on a daily basis and we see how that turned out. You're mad because you involved yourself with someone who truly didn't care for you," Mariah stated dismissively.

Taking the napkin again to wipe her face, she shook her head.

"I'm going to share a story with you. I know you have been led to believe a lot of different things on this situation."

Sitting back in the chair, Coco paused before speaking.

"Sixteen years ago, I had the night of my life with your father and mother. We were living the life of normal grown people, so foolishness was bound to be in the mix of us at some point. The next morning we all sat around the table preparing to eat breakfast, your mother was cooking. A few minutes later a woman walked in the kitchen who I assumed to be your father's side piece. We all enjoyed a few laughs and I happened to make a remark that this woman didn't take too kindly," Coco said smiling.

Knowing that she was referring to Erica, Mariah continued to listen without interrupting her.

"Unfortunately I didn't know she took that comment a little too seriously. My intentions were to apologize after I saw I'd ruffled her feathers with my words. But before I could, she jumped across the counter and smashed a glass coffee mug across my head," Coco said touching the scar that was still very much visible. "Of course I feel that I didn't deserve that, but instead of her stopping there or anyone defusing this reckless situation, they watched her beat me. I mean she literally beat me. I was helpless and very embarrassed. Now... your father never let me explain or even apologize. Instead he fired me and told me to get out of his home. I guess that was just my luck. Anyway I was dealing with an associate who I didn't know would almost cost me my life and he happened to be your father's cousin," Coco said with tears forming in her eyes.

"Somehow your dad heard that I was trying to set him up. I guess in retaliation of what happened between me and this girl. I may have said some reckless things, but not with the intent to see him hurt. Your dad was a very cruel and evil person and he didn't care if I was a part of the situation or not. A few weeks later, I was in my home inside the shower and he broke in. He came into the bathroom and pulled the curtain back. He told me to meet him in the living room."

The tears were now cascading down her cheeks and Mariah could see the hurt in her eyes.

"He had sex with me and"

Pausing again, she took a deep breath and turned her back towards Mariah showing her the reason her life would be changed forever.

Staring in amazement, Mariah choked on her words as she looked at the huge dent in the back of her head. Observing her from the front you wouldn't be able to tell unless she showed you. Her hair was in patches and the gruesome wound looked as if someone caved her head in with a metal bat.

"He shot me in the head after he was done having his way with me. It's like I just blacked out," she mumbled with a painful expression. "He was the last person I remember seeing before I left the earth."

Turning back around, she faced Mariah and could see the sympathy written on her.

"I thought I was dead. I woke up from a coma two years later and I had a beautiful daughter standing next to me," she smiled showing her the long scar across her stomach. "So, yes I raised her to hate, to win, to kill. Regardless of what your father did I never wanted to hurt you all. Even though my daughter suffered. I just want him," Coco stated pulling out another Newport.

"My dad is dead. I never knew anything about this and I doubt if my mother did. You got your wish, he's already in a box."

Lighting her cigarette, Coco broke out into a fit of laughter.

"Dead? Maybe his soul and heart. But physically, he's far from dead and I won't stop until I find him."

"That's not true!" Mariah said on the verge of tears.

"Oh?" Leaning forward, she blew out a mouthful of smoke. "Just look close enough and you will see him. There's a reason his name is Ghost," she mouthed as Frost entered the room.

Looking at her daughter, she stood to her feet.

"Don't kill her, we need all three of them here. I know he'll come," she said with a stern tone.

"I won't."

Watching Coco walk out of the room, Frost placed a pair of thick gloves over her hand.

"It will only hurt while you're awake," she smiled before delivering a hard right fist to Mariah's jaw.

***

Federal Building
Pryor Street

Making her way into the Federal building, she moved swiftly through the metal detectors and headed to her superior's office. Instead of knocking she entered while he was in a conversation on the phone.

Looking at her with an awkward expression, he ended the call. "Something just came up, I'll have to give you a call back."

Hanging up, he removed his glasses, "Where is Rivers?"

"He's situated, sir. I have it under control."

"You left a Federal informant who's under the protection by the DEA alone? Myers, what the hell is wrong with you?" he shouted standing to his feet.

"Sir, there may be more to this story than we can see and I think I can crack this case within the next forty-eight hours on the Ramirez family."

"And we've already discovered that way, Myers. By using the Rivers family. You've done enough and it's a job well done but making any other action could cause us to lose it all in one," McKenny stated.

"Sir, I'm not here to be disputatious. What if I can prove to you that Chance Grey isn't dead?" she asked folding her arms.

"Then I would ask you how in the hell you would figure something like that?"

Pulling out the copy of Frost's birth certificate, she placed it in his face. "This is the hospital's copy of Franchesca Ramirez's birth document the day she was born."

"Okay and what does this prove?"

"The original copy had a signature of Eva Ramirez as her mother. Look at what it says on the clinic's copy."

Placing on his glasses he stared at the name. "And?"

Pulling another piece of paper from her pocket she sat it in front of him.

"What is this?"

"The last ten locations of this woman's whereabouts who's listed as her real mother."

"Myers what significance does this hold to say that Chance Grey is still alive?"

Flipping the paper over on the opposite side, she showed him the same locations.

"Myers, this is all the same."

"Exactly, those are the last ten locations that Chance Grey was spotted from our files."

Reviewing the information again with a close eye, he placed a hand over his mouth.

"She's following him."

Flashing a huge smile, Courtney stood up straight with an arrogant expression.

"Let's say you're right on this. Why would she be in Atlanta?"

"If I were chasing someone, I would want to be in Atlanta where that person's daughters are too."

McKenny agreed with her and crossed his fingers that they were right as a sly smirk crossed his face.

"Give em forty eight hours and I'll have a warrant."

Opening the door to leave, he stopped her.

"Myers! Wait for my call. I can see the look in your eyes. Follow protocol and watch Rivers until you hear from me." McKenny authorized.

"If you know me so well, you shouldn't have to say anything, sir," Courtney replied before leaving out.

If things went according to this plan, everything that she plotted would fall directly into place.

Chapter 18

"I get what you're saying Laylah, but we can't just run around murdering innocent people in order to find her. We need a plan and that starts with getting information on where these people are, first," Stone said trying to ease her tension.

"You don't understand. My mom and stepmother are not going to accept anything less from me. I was raised on handling situations like this. I have to find her before they take matters into their own hands," Laylah stressed, sounding more nervous than anything.

"Laylah, what could they possibly expect out of you? You're only one person. You can't take on the world by yourself," Reeses said standing up.

Shaking her head, "You really don't understand the veracity of this problem," she mouthed.

"I understand that they have high expectations of you, but guess what? You're not with them right now, Laylah. You're with me and we're family. The way I was raised, family looks out for each other, no matter what. Me and Stone are going to be beside you until your sister walks back through that door. Then we're gonna get the fuck out of here. So, I need you to cheer up because everything is going to be okay. We can't win if we're thinking with madness and pain," Reeses reasoned while grabbing ahold of Laylah's hand.

"Okay," Laylah mumbled, as she tried to contain her burning anger.

"Where is the ring I gave you? You haven't been acting like yourself since you stopped wearing it," Reeses asked, making a joke to lighten the mood.

"I'm just not a big fan of jewelry. Mariah has it on."

As Stone typed on the laptop, his mind flashed back as if he was experiencing a case of de ja vu.

As a sudden feeling of nausea rushed through her system, Reeses puked violently on the floor.

"Are you okay?" Laylah asked, as Stone jumped out of the chair. Holding her hand up, she nodded.

"My stomach has been hurting since last night. I think it was something I ate."

"We probably need to get you to a doctor," Stone suggested with a worried expression.

"I'm fine, I just need a little water."

After retrieving her request, he looked at Laylah. "The ring that Reeses gave you? Are you sure that Mariah has it on?"

"I think so, why?" she asked.

Moving quickly towards his duffel bag, Stone quickly unzipped it and began to scan through its contents. Flipping the entire bag over, he rambled in his belongings until he found Justin's Iphone.

"This is why," he said holding the phone in the air as if it answered all their questions.

As both of them looked at him with a confused expression, Stone began to break things down.

"When I first started working for Reeses, I placed a microscopic device on that ring. I connected it to Justin's Iphone in case of critical situations like these. That's how I was able to find you in the Virgin Islands."

"So you can basically track where she is?" Reeses asked, feeling a little hope.

"If she has it on, yes! I'm gonna connect it to the laptop and it should tell us the exact spot she's located," he replied, springing into action.

Praying to herself Laylah hoped that they could receive an answer for Mariah. Protecting her sister was a mission she was born for. Regardless of what Reeses and Stone felt, her heart and skills were big enough to take on the world and plenty more when it came to Mariah. All she needed was an address.

Typing quickly on the computer, Stone tried his best to connect the phone's Find Me app. His anger was starting to rise as he fumbled with the cell numerous times. Just as his frustration was about to make him give in, the information he desperately needed flashed across the screen.

"I got it!"

Jumping to their feet Laylah and Reeses eyes roamed curiously.

"She's in Macon Georgia," he said looking up at them.

***

Virgin Islands

Walking swiftly through the elegant home, Tiffany headed into her master bedroom. Stepping inside her enormous closet, her light green eyes moved around until she found what she was searching for. Pulling the medium sized box from the shelf, she opened it and began to flip through the stack of passports. After finding the correct one she moved down to the titanium safe that sat in her closet wall. After entering the code, she opened the steel door and removed two navy blue Glock 23 handguns. Checking the chambers, she closed the safe and maneuvered to her bed.

Even after sixteen years Tiffany's beauty was still like no other. Her body was still magnificent and tight like the body of a twenty year old. Her long hair now hung past the small of her back and her ambition to be the queen of all the islands was at its peak.

Placing her hair into a ponytail, she pulled a black GA Pro bullet-proof vest from under her mattress. Sitting it on the side of the bed, she made her way back through the hallway.

"I'm going to Atlanta," she said to the man who was walking up the steps.

"What's wrong?" Michael asked seeing the trouble in her face.

"Laylah and Mariah," Tiffany replied dryly.

Hearing his granddaughters' name, his heart started racing as he closed his eyes.

"Please tell me they're okay?"

Instead of giving an answer that she wasn't sure of, she kept it simple. "They need us."

Moving past him down the stairs, Tiffany made her way out to the large backyard. Before opening the glass door she stepped out and spotted Erica. Her silky hair was blowing with the breeze as she stood in the grass watching the waves form on the gigantic beach that sat behind their home.

After closing the distance between them, Tiffany walked up to Erica and greeted her with a kiss.

"We have to go," she said with a straight face.

Looking at her with a raised eyebrow, Erica turned to face her.

"What's going on? What do you mean we have to go?"

"Our daughters need us."

Erica shook her head with disapproval, she folded her arms and a frown wrinkled her beautiful face. "I told you I didn't want them going up there. This job was too dangerous for them. Didn't I tell you that?" she questioned through clenched teeth.

Lowering her gaze, Tiffany stood in silence not wanting to add more fuel to the fire.

"Are my daughters okay?" Erica asked placing a finger under Tiffany's chin to lift her head.

"We need to go," Tiffany repeated staring into her brown eyes.

Picking up her grey Gucci pumps out of the grass, she eyed Tiffany with fire dancing in her pupils.

"I'll deal with you when we come back. Let's go," she stated heading for the house.

During the sixteen years she had been away, she changed. The soft spoken woman who everyone remembered as Erica, no longer lived inside of her. The power struck mind frame she developed was enforced from Jamaica, St Croix, St Thomas to the Virgin Islands. Her temper could rise in a second and the murder rate was rising daily from the orders she issued. After losing Bernard and Ghost to the world, she vowed to herself that God himself wouldn't be able to touch another member of her family. That was a promise that she was willing to enforce by any means necessary.

***

Macon Georgia
7:30pm

After watching the black Maserati pull inside the gated home, Courtney wasted no time stepping out of her vehicle. Dressed in black, she headed to the bushes that sat on the side of the humongous house.

All she needed to do was get close enough to snap a picture of Eva or Frost, in order to have the warrant signed by the judge immediately. Valuable time was being wasted and in order for the plan she'd devised to push through, the Ramirez family would have to fall.

Looking at the nine foot wall in front of her, she jumped and grabbed the ledge. Courtney lifted her head slightly and stared at the secluded section of the home. Taking her chances, she lifted herself up and leaped over. Pushing her back against the side of the home she peeped around the corner and saw the guards who patrolled around the perimeter. Spotting the black Maserati, her heart began to race as Eva climbed out of the passenger seat.

Snatching her camera from the hip, she quickly snapped four pictures of the notorious queen pin. Looking at the woman who got out on the driver's side, she paused. Her face was familiar but she knew if you were in the same vehicle with Eva Ramirez than she had to be someone important. Placing the camera on her she took a few pictures before they disappeared into the entrance of the home.

Viewing the pictures on her small Sony screen, she never spotted the Spanish guard approaching her from behind.

"Can I help you?" he asked with folded arms.

Turning around, she didn't hesitate to send a vicious kick to his groin. Watching him kneel over in pain she landed a punch directly to the center of his nose. As Courtney prepared herself to jump back over the wall a pair of strong hands grabbed her and slammed her to the ground. Pulling the cuffs off her waist, he placed them on her wrist as she struggled to break free.

"Feisty chica!" the guard smiled lifting her up.

"Get the fuck off me!" she screamed, kicking her feet wildly.

As the first henchmen regain the feeling back in his nuts, he stood to his feet and backhanded Courtney viciously. Grabbing her by the hair, they walked her around the corner and headed to the front of the home.

***

"Ma'am, de hace a problemas," a guard stated stepping into the living area interrupting Eva and Coco's conversation.

Standing to her feet Eva watched as the two men walked in pushing Courtney to the floor.

As she looked up into Eva's eyes, Courtney couldn't help but grow nervous. Eva's menacing gaze felt as if she would burn a hole straight through the center of Courtney's head.

"Who are you?" she asked as the entire room stood back in silence.

Not wanting to expose her hand, Courtney remained quiet.

"You have to be someone if you're standing in my living room. Where did she come from?" Eva asked turning her attention to one of the guards.

"I caught her on the side of the house taking pictures with this camera," he stated while passing it to Eva, "After I confronted her, she attacked me and tried to leap over the wall like a ninja or something," he added while holding his bloody nose.

Raising her hand to silence him, Eva viewed the photos with a disturbed expression. Glaring at Courtney, she took her seat and sparked a cigarette.

"She's a fucking cop," Eva said in a calm tone.

Removing their pistols quickly, she stopped them before anyone could place a bullet in the back of her head.

"I want to know why you're on my property taking pictures. Obviously you're here for a reason I presume."

Courtney knew that moving alone was officially the biggest mistake she could have ever made. There was no way to call in for back up and her life was now on the line. The guards looked as if they were anxious to take care of her with brutal punishment and she saw no way to get herself out of the turmoil that was presenting itself.

"You snuck on private property, assaulted my guard and now you sit in front of me with nothing to say."

"If you harm me in any type of way, this entire place will be seized and everyone who stands with you will be arrested within the next forty eight hours," she replied, hoping to cause a little nervousness with the comment.

142

"Thank you for the heads up. Take her upstairs with the other one," Eva commanded with a nonchalant expression.

Grabbing Courtney by the hair, a guard pulled her towards the steps. Dragging her to the top he walked into a room and placed her in a chair. After slapping a piece of tape on her mouth he began to tie her to the seat.

"Behave yourself or you will die quicker than expected," he said before walking out.

Shrinking in fear of his words she stared at the woman in the chair across from her. Her face was severely swollen and by the way her head dangled you could tell that she was unconscious.

Tapping her feet to see if the girl would move didn't get any reaction. The handcuffs on her wrist were starting to bite and there was no way for her to climb out of the shitty situation. All she could do was wait and see what the devilish woman had planned for her.

Chris Green

Chapter 18

10:30pm

Spotting the black Maserati pulling out of the parking lot, Stone and Laylah prepared themselves for the task that was at hand.

"Sue, are you ready?" Reeses asked through the earpiece.

"I told you the first time, I got it. This uniform starting to itch my ass," she replied loudly.

Shaking her head, Reeses looked at Stone.

"Are you sure you want this bitch to be the one doing this?"

"We don't have a choice," he responded while watching Sue pull up to the gate.

"Now!" Laylah said stepping out of the vehicle with her guns tucked inside her holster. Grabbing his AR-15 assault rifle, he jumped out of the car directly behind her.

***

Pulling the car in front of the huge gate, Sue watched as the man walked to her passenger side window with a odd expression on his face. She rolled down the window, the man lowered his head.

"Can I help you?" he asked with a thick Spanish tone.

"I deliver a plate for Ms. Ramirez. She order spicy chicken, four eggrolls, one shrimp rice"

Waving his hand as if he wanted her to shut up, he buzzed the gate giving her access to go in. Before he could straighten his back, Laylah plunged her hand held hunting knife into his throat twice. Seeing the life exit his body, she pulled her Glock from its holster and entered the driveway with Stone behind her.

Tapping the infer-red beam on the side of his weapon, he released four loud shots that eliminated the two guards who moved towards them.

Boc! Boc! Boc! Boc!

Seeing the intensity of the situation, Sue reversed the car and smashed off heading in the opposite direction.

Drawing near the entrance of the home, a guard opened the door and caught the edge of Laylah's knife through his navel. Cringing in pain, she leveled her pistol.

Boc!

The vicious slug ripped through the bottom of his chin causing him to crumble to the ground.

As they advanced into the home, several gunshots rang out, missing Stone's head by an inch.

Boc! Boc! Boc! Boc!

"I knew you would come Laylah," Frost said as she stood in the living area aiming her pistol. While standing behind the wall across from Laylah, Stone tried to peek around the sharp corner. The bullets Frost sent next chiseled chunks out of the brick, giving him the indication not to try anything foolish.

"You're my sister, Laylah. We can handle this a little more discreetly."

Laylah stepped out from behind the wall with her pistols aimed. She stared at Frost with her trigger finger ready to release the entire clip. Her resemblance of their father was undeniable, she even possessed his same cold glare.

"I knew this would end soon. I've waited a long time to see exactly how good you were," she stated throwing her pistol to the floor.

"Stone, find my sister," Laylah said while placing her guns on the floor.

Watching the two standoff, he knew that something above his lead was taking place. Gripping his assault rifle, he eased past them heading slowly up the stairs. The look Frost gave him sent chills down his spine as he left them in the living room.

Frost wasted no time launching towards Laylah with the large blade she'd pulled from her pocket. Laylah Side stepped her attack and delivered a vicious elbow to the side of Frost's rib cage and removed her own knife.

Swinging the blade with extreme force, Laylah moved backwards trying her best to dodge the sharp point. With a high kick to Frost's wrist, the knife sailed towards the wall, hitting the floor. Advancing forward, she aimed her steel towards the center of Frost's throat. Her attempt missed allowing her sister to place her in a deadly chokehold.

"You can't beat me! Today will be your last time opening your eyes!" Frost said with malice in her heart as she tightened the firm lock on Laylah's neck.

***

After walking through three different rooms of the home, Stone stopped at the last door and entered with his gun raised. Hitting the light switch, he spotted Mariah bound to a thick chair. He started to cut the thick plastic wire that was wrapped around her body.

Moving her feet in desperate need of help, Courtney made enough noise that Stone jerked his head up, looking into her pleading eyes.

"What the fuck?' he mumbled to himself wondering how she ended up in the same predicament.

After cutting Mariah from the entrapment, he prepared to pick her up.

"Don't leave her, Stone," Mariah whispered through her swollen lips. "It wouldn't be right."

Looking back over at Courtney, the hatred still weighed heavy in his heart for her shooting him, but he knew that Mariah was right. Allah would never forgive him if he could have saved a life but chose not to.

Rushing quickly over to her, he snatched the tape from her mouth, before cutting her loose.

"Thank you so much. I promise"

"Yeah, whatever. I'm still not letting that shit you did to me slide." He said using the pistol on his waist to bust the handcuffs. "Let's go!"

Placing Mariah over his shoulders, they made their way out of the room.

***

After beating Frost profusely with her fist, Laylah stood over her as she laid on the floor. Picking up her knife, she raised it ready to plunge it inside of her heart. The demons inside of her head were racing and her low, slanted, green eyes were filled with murder.

Before she could end Frost's life for good, one last henchman stepped around the corner pulling his trigger. The bullet slammed into Laylah forcing her to the floor, just as Stone and Courtney came down the steps with Mariah.

Without hesitating, Courtney grabbed Stone's pistol and released the entire clip into the man's torso.

Bloc! Bloc! Bloc! Bloc! Bloc! Bloc! Bloc! Bloc!

Running to Laylah's side she pulled up her shirt staring at the slug that was lodged into the bulletproof vest. Witnessing Laylah blink her eyes she helped her up slowly.

Grateful that she was okay Stone closed his eyes thanking Allah for his mercy.

"We gotta get the fuck out of here!"

***

As she sat in the car, Reeses couldn't do anything but worry until she spotted them coming out of the driveway. Her energy was pumping so fast, she fumbled to get the car crunk. Starting the engine she pulled up and stopped directly in front of them.

Placing Mariah in the backseat, Laylah climbed in beside her. Reeses eyes widened, seeing Courtney get in behind them. Pulling her 9mm in a flash she placed it to the center of her head.

"What in the fuck is this bitch doing here?" she snarled with her finger gripping the trigger tightly.

"Baby, stop! We found her with Mariah. She has nothing to do with this," Stone said jumping in the front seat to grab ahold of her hand.

"What makes you so sure of that? She's the reason all of this shit is happening to us now."

Reeses was on the verge of tears for wanting to pull the trigger so bad. Her hands began to tremble as Stone eased the gun from her possession.

Courtney sat there looking totally clueless as Reeses stared her down with hatred.

"Reeses, we have to go," Stone interjected, trying to get her to focus.

Turning back around in her seat, she smashed on the gas pedal leaving the street full of smoke. The drive back down to Atlanta was awkwardly silent. Looking through her rearview, Reeses glanced at Laylah who held Mariah close to her as if she would disappear. Switching her vision over to Courtney, she slowed the car down on the expressway, hitting the hazard lights.

Turning around, she looked at her with disgust, "Get the fuck out of my car. We're fifteen minutes from Atlanta. Shouldn't be that much of a walk," she spat.

"Reeses, we're on the middle of the highway," Stone said trying to show a little sympathy.

"Are you fucking this bitch or something? She's probably about to get me a life sentence in a few days. I said get the fuck out!"

Nodding her head, Courtney opened the door and stepped out on the expressway. As the car pulled away, she couldn't help but release all the tears she had held back through this entire ordeal. Her life had been seconds from ending and the ones who she was working against swooped in to her rescue. That was the last sign she needed to make her decision. There was nothing that would change her mind.

Chapter 19

5:32am

As she stirred from her sleep, Reeses rolled over to find Tiffany sitting at the edge of her bed.

"Hey baby girl," she said with a warm tone.

Moving the covers from her body, she wrapped her arms around her aunt hugging tightly.

"I can't believe you're here," Reeses uttered with tears forming in her eyes. "Where's Laylah and Mariah?"

"I have to send them back home. I made a bad decision by letting them come up here. But I did accomplish one thing. Finding you," she replied with a beautiful smile.

"I hope you're not mad at me. I never meant to put them into any danger. If I would've listened and left when they warned me the first time, I would have never been in this predicament."

Touching her cheek, Tiffany shook her head. "I could never be mad at you, Rinesha. You look so much like Jimmie, I'm so sorry I let you down. It may seem like things are hard for you but staying up here is not an option. After your court date, I expect you to be on the first flight to the islands. You have to come home with family, baby. It's the only way I can sleep at night."

Nodding, she embraced Tiffany in another hug. "I understand, Auntie."

Kissing her forehead, Tiffany moved past Stone, who stood by the room door and left quickly as she came. Observing the disturbed look on her face, he moved closer and took a seat beside Reeses.

"Are you gonna be okay?" he asked, placing a hand on her shoulder.

Looking at him with sadness written on her expression, she faced him. "What are we going to do now?"

Catching him off guard with the question he thought hard before answering. "We're gonna do exactly what we suppose to. We're going to handle your trial and I'm going to make sure you catch that flight to make it safely to your family."

What about you?'

"I'll be okay. I was actually thinking about going to law school and finishing college. My record was cleared last year, so it could actually be a new start for me."

Getting out of the bed, she opened her Saint Laurent purse, pulling out a small brown paper bag. Tossing it into his lap, she folded her arms.

Looking down with a speculative glance he opened it and poured the contents into his hand. Staring at the two pregnancy sticks that read positive, he raised his head to meet her stern gaze.

Getting up he moved towards her with open arms. "It's alright, ma. I'm right here, no matter what. We're going to be just fine," he assured, placing a smooch on her forehead.

***

Cobb County Courtroom

"This woman's innocent looks is only a disguise, Judge Franklin. She's trying to disentangle herself from the critical problem that's upon her and I'm afraid it's too late. We have criminal charges of conspiracy that she is facing. It's sad say that a woman at this age could even devise a plan that's involved innocent people who weren't aware of her actions to take over the Smyrna and Atlanta Georgia area with drugs and murder. We cannot pacify her in this situation just because she's nineteen years old, looks can be very deceiving. Don't let her beguile you to believe that she couldn't pull off a scheme so brilliant." The Assistant District Attorney said to the jury.

"Mr. Harvey, you may proceed."

"Thank you, your Honor I would like to start off first by stating that my client doesn't have any criminal record what so ever. The state is literally trying to use her father's history against her to build a case and that's ridiculous. Now we've heard every story in the book to discredit Ms. Rivers on her innocence, but we haven't seen any physical proof, yet."

"I object your Honor, we have two federal witnesses that are present here today."

Hearing the statement made Reeses' flesh crawl. She knew that trusting Courtney was a big mistake and now she regretted not pulling the trigger when she had the chance. Her mind still couldn't stomach the fact of her own brother, the one she cherished was ready to give her up so he wouldn't have to suffer anymore prison time.

"Well, hearing the facts of the case I would have to side with Mr. Harvey for now. Even though you stated that we have witnesses, we still haven't seen any tangible or physical evidence that shows Ms. Rivers being a criminal. Now I've been a judge for over twenty four years and I understand that you can never judge a book by its cover, but her record speaks for a lot. Everything the State has placed against her is only accusations of things her family has committed in the past. One or two apples doesn't spoil the entire bunch, so I think that you may need to proceed with getting the witnesses on the stand to paint a more vivid picture of what we have going on in this court room at the time, Mr. Paulk."

"Right away, Your Honor. The State would like to call Agent Courtney Myers to the stand."

Sitting in the crowd, blending in with the civilians, Stone watched as she made her way inside the court room. Her nervous look said that she was very uncomfortable with what was taking place as she made her way to the front.

"Ms. Myers, do you swear to state the truth, nothing else but the truth within this case?" The DA questioned holding the Holy Bible in front of her.

Placing her hand on top of it, she took a deep breath and let her eyes roam towards the jury.

"I do."

Gripping the pen in her hand tightly, Reeses sat back with murderous thoughts running vividly through her brain. As if he sensed the tension, Harvey placed a hand on Reeses shoulder and encouraged her to relax.

"Very well, can you please inform the courtroom on your job description?" Paulk asked with a curious stare.

"I'm an agent for the DEA and my job is to investigate notorious drug dealers and leak their operations."

"Okay and can you tell us how Ms. Rivers fits into this subject?"

"I don't know," she lied with a straight face.

Snapping his head around quickly, he adjusted his tie. "Let me rephrase that question for you so we can get a better understanding. What form of evidence have you obtained on the defendant since you've began your investigation."

"Nothing," Courtney replied in a dry tone while looking at Reeses.

"Agent Myers, do you hear what you're saying?" the attorney asked in an angry tone.

"Objection your honor he can't antagonize the witness to say what he wants," Harvey stated standing to his feet.

Looking into Courtney's eyes Reeses cracked a smile.

"Paulk! Keep it clean," Judge Franklin said sternly.

"Ms. Rivers is on your caseload, Agent Myers? Is there anything you can tell us about this investigation?" he pleaded in a sincere tone.

"I was assigned to investigate her. I have accumulated no evidence for my own eyes to say that she is distributing anything. This case has caused a physical and mental disturbance upon me and I'm afraid that I can't come up here to fabricate a story to help you with your job, sir. My time is up," she said glaring at the courtroom.

"Ms. Meyers, what are you saying?" Judge Franklin asked pushing the glasses on the bridge of his nose up.

"Removing her badge, she laid it on top of the flat surface in front of her. "I quit, may I step down now?"

"You're free to leave, Ms. Myers," the judge confirmed.

"Your Honor, I'm not too good with telling stories, but it seems as if this is coming to a close. My client is tired and I think this case is starting to become a little confusing."

"We still have another witness," the DA butted in with hostility in his tone.

"My patience is running thin," Franklin replied.

"Can we please bring the next witness in?"

Watching the State's assistant walk over to Paulk. She whispered in his ear and stepped back with an awkward frown.

"Your Honor, I was just informed that the Federal witness has fled the courthouse. If you could give us a two hour recess we can locate him to wrap this case up."

"Overruled. I will not continue to hold the jury up with your tainted methods and insufficient evidence. Does the jury need to deliberate or do we already have a verdict?" the judge asked looking at the twelve seated members.

A white man dressed in a two piece suit stood to his feet.

"We do your honor. We the jury find, Rinesha Rivers on count one of drug trafficking. Not guilty."

Looking back at Stone, Reeses winked her eye.

The jury continued to read off on the next seven charges and all but the last came to her satisfaction.

"We the jury find Rinesha Rivers on the count of conspiracy to manipulate a drug operation. Guilty."

"Shit!" she cursed lowering her head.

"Their only doing this because of what Agent Myers stated at your preliminary hearing. It was no way around it, just let me talk to the judge," Harvey said standing to his feet.

"Your Honor, my client has discovered that she is pregnant. In the next seven in a half months she would be preparing to give birth to her first child, she has no criminal history. Is there any way that we can bring this down to five years on paper?"

"I object, your Honor. She's guilty of this charge and it carries anywhere from five to ten years, probation is out of the question," Paulk said with authority.

"I'm at liberty to agree with Mr. Paulk on this Harvey. I will not be able to grant the probation. Young lady, this is serious situation and I hope that you understand how important your life is especially when you speak about bringing a child into this world. I have a daughter that's older than you. I'm going to sentence you to a five serve two. We will make sure you have the proper procedure for your child's birth and I wish you the best of luck."

"I'll try to have you out in one," Harvey said as the bailiff approached Reeses to place her in cuffs.

Turning around to look at Stone one last time. He mumbled the words 'I love you' before she was escorted to the back. Her mind couldn't help but think about the move Courtney and Justin pulled in the end. She knew that the River's name would always stay on top no matter what occurred. It was natural to be in their blood. The same ambition that she knew would pump through her child's veins.

Placing her in a holding tank, the officers closed the door as she sat down. Thinking about her major scheme she couldn't help but smile and wait for her release.

Chapter 20

Alto Women's Facility
One month later

After reading Stone's sweet letter, Reeses placed it back inside the envelope and sat it on the edge of her bed. Adjusting to prison was a little difficult, especially when she was carrying a child with her. The support of loved ones was the best thing she could ask for while doing her time. Her commissary books were overloaded and visitation every week definitely kept a wide smile on her face. Word through a reliable source told her that Justin and Courtney were on the run for refusing to cooperate during the trial. Mariah was doing everything in her power to get her out within the next few months but hit a rocky road with every turn she took and Laylah made it her business to show up to every visitation along with Stone. Within the past four weeks, Stone established three businesses including a nice pizza and pasta eatery that sat in the middle of downtown Atlanta.

Her thoughts was cut short as the officer reappeared at the door. "Rivers, you got another letter, lil' mama," the older woman said sliding it under the door.

Standing to her feet she rubbed the small pudge in her belly before moving to pick it up. Looking at the senders section there was nothing but a small snowflake postage with the initials F.R. by the side of it. Staring at it with a weird expression, Reeses opened it pulling out the single piece of paper. Scanning it with her yes she began to read.

Reeses,

It took a minute for me to gather everything I wanted to say, but now I think that I am ready. First off I pray that you are doing alright in that prison facility. It's a cruel place behind the walls of the system and I know sometimes it can drive your emotions around like a roller coaster. My advice: difficulties come with everything we go through so never let it pressure you. Besides I need you in perfect condition for the day you come home. Regardless of you having truly nothing

to do with this situation you're considered guilty by association. My lovely sisters are playing a deadly game that's going to cause a lot of innocent lives to be lost. I don't think you're aware of what's going on so I will fill you in. The word family is deeper than you think, it may mean loved ones and close friends to you. But in our dictionary it means enemy. For years our generations have battled with each other to remain on top of this empire that was once united. Unfortunately my father, your uncle had a different agenda. So I don't want you to take anything personally when I say this... You're gonna die. I'm going to torture you along with the other two until I feel a sense of satisfaction. Then I will place a bullet in between your eyes, it's just the price of being family, in the end we will suffer the same fate I just refuse to be first. I'll be seeing you very soon.
Frost

Folding up the paper, she placed it neatly under her pillow and laid back on the bed. Tossing the treacherous words from Frost around in her head caused goosebumps to rise on her skin. Not because of fear, it was from being challenged. Closing her eyes, Teeses thought about the way she would bury Frostb in a six foot hole.

***

Overlook Atlanta
10:45 pm

Sitting in the living room of the small apartment, Tremaine took a hit of the crystal cocaine and passed it to Slick.

"You gotta be careful my nigga. That shit will have you tweaking," he said with a short chuckle.

"I tweak no matter how good the dope is bruh," Slick replied taking a line up the nasal pipe. "So when you think you gone be ready to get back out in them streets and get that paper like we use to?"

"I don't know, fool. Shit has been extremely ugly lately. I'm still on probation for shit we did eight years ago. My baby's mom slid me on this child support, shit. I'm definitely not trying to go back to prison. It's hard behind them walls when a mufucka won't show yo' ass no love," he said keeping it real.

"It comes with the streets, nigga. There ain't no gangsta out there that ain't took chances to make the shit happen how they wanted. Its rules to this shit. If I'm telling you we can make some chedda, real easy paper. Then you know I'm telling the truth."

Taking a swig of his Colt 45 beer, he tried his best to soak up the weak ass game Slick was spitting.

"What exactly are you talking about?"

"I'm talking about some millions, three or more. Guaranteed."

"Millions? Nigga, you must be trying to hit a fucking bank or some shit?' Tremaine said thinking that he was over exaggerating.

"No bank. Just one person."

"Who?"

"Reeses," Slick stated with a blank face.

Hearing the name made his stomach turn. "I can't fuck with Rinesha, bro. I got mad respect for Jimmie and that little girl is like a niece to me."

"Nigga, Jimmie is in a fucking box and she ain't yo niece, she's mine. So what the fuck you scared of?"

"I ain't scared, bro. It just wouldn't feel right, just let me think on it a while."

"Sitting back thinking about the shit ain't gone get us nowhere. It's easy, we run down on this bitch and we strike. Simple. The girl is nineteen trying to play in this dope game like she a street, nigga. Ain't no rules to this shit! If you get yo nose wiped, chop it up and charge it to the game. That's how we been playing," Slick said with an emotional fury.

"Let's just think this shit through, bro. You know I'm always down to ride with you. But if we do it, it has to be done right," Tremaine lied to ease the heated tension he felt approaching.

"I've done so much fucking waiting that I growed a full beard. We can ride out tomorrow. All you gotta do is follow my lead."

Nodding in compliance, Tremaine slipped a cigarette between his lips and torched the end.

"You got any cash on some more coke or what?'

"I'm sitting here tweaking about paper and you asking me do I got some on the powder."

Tremaine laughed then inhaled deeply on the tobacco.

"Did you hear that?" Slick asked jerking his head looking at the bathroom door.

"I told you that shit will have you bugging. I ain't heard shit," he replied.

Slick glanced around the living room with a disturbed look on his face before returning to his seat on the couch. The negative vibes that Tremaine picked up on from observing his friend were so strong that he found an excuse to leave.

"I got fifty dollars on me. I'm about to slide over to Doe's apartment and snatch us some nose candy," he mentioned while heading to the door.

"That shit don't take all day either man," Slick said leaning his head back on the couch.

Shuffling a wicked plan through his mind, Slick knew that going for Reeses would take everything he had. The way she moved around the city as if she owned it caused him to toot his nose up in anger. He sat up straight as he heard the loud clicking sound again. Digging a finger in his ear, he looked around before standing up.

"I need to lay down," he mumbled to himself heading into the bedroom.

Slick laid back on the bed staring directly into the light of the ceiling fan. Closing his eyes, he took a deep breath enjoying the cool breeze. The loud clicking that had sounded off in his ear and forced his eyes back open was now clear.

The sight of Ghost standing in his bedroom doorway drained all forms of gangsta from his body. Ghost's dark pupils spelt death and the large gun he held was aimed directly for Slick's head. His finger pulled back the hammer slowly and that dreadful click sent chills through his body.

"No one cheats the grim reaper, nigga," Ghost smiled before popping his burner.

Bloc! Bloc! Bloc! Bloc! Bloc!

Watching Slick crumble back on the bed, he stepped closer staring down into Slick's open eyes. Placing the barrel to his head, Ghost released one last bullet before walking out of the apartment.

***

One year and six months later
Alto Women's Facility

Reeses sat quietly in the holding cell of the women's prison, in deep thought. Her mind pondered everyday on her release and now it was finally here.

As the cell door slid back, a young female stuck her head inside. "Rivers, it's time. Their ready for you."

Standing, she walked out of the cell into the processing area.

"I just have to get your fingerprints and you're free to go," the young woman informed Reeses with a humble smile.

Seeing that Reeses wasn't over ecstatic about her release, she eyed her curiosity.

"I know you happy to be leaving this place, my ass wouldn't be able to stop moving."

"Spending just a little time behind here will teach you a lot. You learn to slow down and not to be in too much of a rush for anything," Reeses replied with a wink.

"I can definitely feel that."

Finishing her prints, she gave Reeses a napkin to clean her hands. "Well girl, you're free to go. Stay safe."

Staring at the woman's dull correctional officer uniform, she reached down for the pen that sat on the counter. Scribbling a number on the paper, she handed it to her.

"Get up with me in a couple of weeks. I'll make it worth your while," Reeses said heading for the door.

"What do you mean?" she asked with a confused expression.

Reeses stopped in her tracks and looked back. "Sometimes it's not about what you know, it's who you know. I took a lot of things for granted. And a lot of things I was granted was taken. Sad to say they left me one thing. Money! Quit your job and I'll see you in two weeks," she responded before walking out into the free world.

Chapter 21

The sun beamed down on her dark grey eyes as she stepped out into the parking lot. Spotting Stone and Laylah standing by the parked 2019 white Range Rover, she made her way towards them. After closing the distance she embraced Laylah in a firm hug.

"All this visiting I been doing, you owe me a trip to the James Patterson book convention that's coming up," Laylah smiled with joy.

"Right about now, you can get whatever the hell you want," Reeses snickered.

Glancing at Stone, he smiled. "Hey beautiful."

Reeses wrapped her arms around him, placed a warm kiss on his lips and buried her head into his chest.

"Did you miss me?"

"Every second," he replied.

"We'll see," she teased grabbing his manhood slyly.

Looking down, she stared into a pair of light grey eyes that resembled her own. Her curly long hair was placed in two afro puffs and her Gucci overalls made her look even more adorable. Bending down, her baby wasted no time embracing her.

"I love you too, Keniyah," she smiled placing numerous kisses on her cheeks.

After strapping her in the car seat, they all climbed in into the vehicle and away from the prison's parking lot.

"So, what's the news," Reeses asked while sitting in the back playing with the baby.

"Business has been excellent, I talked to Harvey last week and he told me that if you complete a year with no new charges they will suspend the balance on your parole.

"What about the flight?"

"The plane leaves for the island around nine tonight," Stone confirmed.

Nodding her head she pulled out the letter she'd received from Frost. Not only had she thought day in and day out about the vicious threats she delivered but she'd patiently waited to make sure they could meet to resolve the deadly issue.

"And Frost?" she questioned with her eyes still glued to the paper. "I've been working hard on finding her. I wish I could've finished her that night in the living room. She's playing the tough role but she knows that it's not just a walk in the park," Laylah said while keeping her eyes on road.

"That bitch has a death wish, we have more important things to focus on. The Feds will be on our heels if we make one mistake. You have to restrain yourself for the time being until you get that opportunity," Stone reminded her.

"It's important when you take your time to write me while I'm in prison to let me know that you're gonna murder me. Frost is very outspoken, that bitch needs to die as soon as possible," Reeses fumed not caring about the threat of the authorities.

"In due time, for right now we have to get you down to the islands. You have a job to do," Laylah said.

"And what's that?"

"You're in charge of Jamaica, everyone's waiting on your arrival."

Holding her daughter's hand, Reeses stared out of the clear window wondering what lies ahead. Locking down half of Atlanta was one thing but controlling an entire island was guaranteed to be a daunting task.

***

Queens, New York

After pulling in to her four bedroom home, Chelsea stepped out of her vehicle and made her way inside.

"Dustin?" she called out for her husband after entering the front door.

Not receiving an answer, she headed upstairs to find the rooms empty. Chelsea walked back down to the main floor of the house and headed off to his usual hangout spot. Opening the back door, he sat in a comfortable fold out chair with a white owl blunt in between his lips.

"Hey baby. How was your day?" she asked planting two kisses on his left cheekbone.

"Smoking my life away. What about you?" he replied grabbing a handful of her juicy backside.

"Stressful, I'm ready to break out of these scrubs and grab a hot shower."

"You really thinking about doing something like that without me?"

"I can only wait so long, I feel so yucky."

"I have to finish cleaning out that damn shed. What the hell is all of that anyway?"

"There's a few things from when we moved but most of it is from your apartment in Georgia. You need to throw those boxes away, that stuff is like fifteen years old."

"Good, that makes it easy for me. By the time you get out of the shower I should be naked in the bed," he smiled while walking off toward the huge yard.

Shaking her head, she giggled to herself and headed inside.

Opening the shed doors, he looked around at all the dusty boxes.

"Goddamn Chelsea, you should've just let this shit get auctioned off or something," he yelled knowing that she couldn't hear him.

Opening one of the brown cardboard lids, he glanced inside. He slowly pulled out the all black jacket. Shaking it caused the pistol in the pocket to hit the ground.

Looking down, he picked up the white pearl handled Glock 40. His mind instantly flashed back as if his old soul was placed back into his body.

"Ghost," he said, just above a whisper.

Dropping the jacket on the floor, he tucked the gun on the side of his hip and rushed towards the house.

"Baby, is something wrong?" Chelsea asked, seeing him speed through the back door.

"I have to go."

"Dustin, what's the problem? What do you mean you have to go?"

Looking around for a second, he remained quiet.

"Honey, you're scaring me. Please say something!"
"I remember what happened," Shadow said, before leaving out the front door.

To Be Continued...
True Savage 7
Coming Soon

Submission Guideline

Submit the first three chapters of your completed manuscript to ldpsubmissions@gmail.com, subject line: Your book's title. The manuscript must be in a .doc file and sent as an attachment. Document should be in Times New Roman, double spaced and in size 12 font. Also, provide your synopsis and full contact information. If sending multiple submissions, they must each be in a separate email.

Have a story but no way to send it electronically? You can still submit to LDP/Ca$h Presents. Send in the first three chapters, written or typed, of your completed manuscript to:

LDP: Submissions Dept
Po Box 870494
Mesquite, Tx 75187

DO NOT send original manuscript. Must be a duplicate.

Provide your synopsis and a cover letter containing your full contact information.

Thanks for considering LDP and Ca$h Presents.

Chris Green

Coming Soon from Lock Down Publications/Ca$h Presents

BOW DOWN TO MY GANGSTA

By **Ca$h**

TORN BETWEEN TWO

By **Coffee**

BLOOD STAINS OF A SHOTTA **III**

By **Jamaica**

STEADY MOBBIN **III**

By **Marcellus Allen**

BLOOD OF A BOSS **V**

By **Askari**

LOYAL TO THE GAME **IV**

LIFE OF SIN II

By **T.J. & Jelissa**

A DOPEBOY'S PRAYER **II**

By **Eddie "Wolf" Lee**

IF LOVING YOU IS WRONG… **III**

LOVE ME EVEN WHEN IT HURTS **II**

By **Jelissa**

TRUE SAVAGE **VII**

By **Chris Green**

BLAST FOR ME **III**

A BRONX TALE III

DUFFLE BAG CARTEL

By **Ghost**

ADDICTIED TO THE DRAMA **III**

By **Jamila Mathis**

168

LIPSTICK KILLAH **III**

WHAT BAD BITCHES DO **III**

KILL ZONE **II**

By **Aryanna**

THE COST OF LOYALTY **II**

By **Kweli**

SHE FELL IN LOVE WITH A REAL ONE **II**

By **Tamara Butler**

RENEGADE BOYS **III**

By **Meesha**

CORRUPTED BY A GANGSTA **IV**

By **Destiny Skai**

A GANGSTER'S CODE **III**

By **J-Blunt**

KING OF NEW YORK IV

RISE TO POWER II

By **T.J. Edwards**

GORILLAS IN THE BAY II

De'Kari

THE STREETS ARE CALLING II

Duquie Wilson

KINGPIN KILLAZ III

Hood Rich

STEADY MOBBIN' **III**

Marcellus Allen

SINS OF A HUSTLA II

ASAD

CASH MONEY HOES

Nicole Goosby

Chris Green

TRIGGADALE II
Elijah R. Freeman
MARRIED TO A BOSS 2…
By Destiny Skai & Chris Green

Available Now
RESTRAINING ORDER I & II
By CA$H & Coffee
LOVE KNOWS NO BOUNDARIES I II & III
By Coffee
RAISED AS A GOON I, II, III & IV
BRED BY THE SLUMS I, II, III
BLAST FOR ME I & II
ROTTEN TO THE CORE I III
A BRONX TALE I, II
By Ghost
LAY IT DOWN I & II
LAST OF A DYING BREED
BLOOD STAINS OF A SHOTTA I & II
By Jamaica
LOYAL TO THE GAME
LOYAL TO THE GAME II
LOYAL TO THE GAME III
LIFE OF SIN
By TJ & Jelissa
BLOODY COMMAS I & II
SKI MASK CARTEL I II & III
KING OF NEW YORK I II,III

170

RISE TO POWER

By **T.J. Edwards**
IF LOVING HIM IS WRONG…I & II
LOVE ME EVEN WHEN IT HURTS
By **Jelissa**
WHEN THE STREETS CLAP BACK I & II III
By **Jibril Williams**
A DISTINGUISHED THUG STOLE MY HEART I II & III
LOVE SHOULDN'T HURT I II III
RENEGADE BOYS I & II
By **Meesha**
A GANGSTER'S CODE I & II
By J-Blunt
PUSH IT TO THE LIMIT
By **Bre' Hayes**
BLOOD OF A BOSS **I, II, III & IV**
By **Askari**
THE STREETS BLEED MURDER **I, II & III**
THE HEART OF A GANGSTA I II& III
By **Jerry Jackson**
CUM FOR ME
CUM FOR ME 2
CUM FOR ME 3
CUM FOR ME 4
An **LDP Erotica Collaboration**
BRIDE OF A HUSTLA **I II & II**
THE FETTI GIRLS **I, II& III**
CORRUPTED BY A GANGSTA I, II & III

By **Destiny Skai**

WHEN A GOOD GIRL GOES BAD

By **Adrienne**

A GANGSTER'S REVENGE **I II III & IV**

THE BOSS MAN'S DAUGHTERS

THE BOSS MAN'S DAUGHTERS II

THE BOSSMAN'S DAUGHTERS III

THE BOSSMAN'S DAUGHTERS IV

THE BOSS MAN'S DAUGHTERS **V**

A SAVAGE LOVE **I & II**

BAE BELONGS TO ME

A HUSTLER'S DECEIT I, II

WHAT BAD BITCHES DO I, II

By **Aryanna**

A KINGPIN'S AMBITON

A KINGPIN'S AMBITION **II**

I MURDER FOR THE DOUGH

By **Ambitious**

TRUE SAVAGE

TRUE SAVAGE II

TRUE SAVAGE **III**

TRUE SAVAGE **IV**

TRUE SAVAGE **V**

TRUE SAVAGE **VI**

By **Chris Green**

A DOPEBOY'S PRAYER

By **Eddie "Wolf" Lee**

THE KING CARTEL **I, II & III**

By **Frank Gresham**

172

THESE NIGGAS AIN'T LOYAL **I, II & III**

By **Nikki Tee**

GANGSTA SHYT **I II &III**

By **CATO**

THE ULTIMATE BETRAYAL

By **Phoenix**

BOSS'N UP **I , II & III**

By **Royal Nicole**

I LOVE YOU TO DEATH

By Destiny J

I RIDE FOR MY HITTA

I STILL RIDE FOR MY HITTA

By **Misty Holt**

LOVE & CHASIN' PAPER

By **Qay Crockett**

TO DIE IN VAIN

SINS OF A HUSTLA

By **ASAD**

BROOKLYN HUSTLAZ

By **Boogsy Morina**

BROOKLYN ON LOCK I & II

By **Sonovia**

GANGSTA CITY

By **Teddy Duke**

A DRUG KING AND HIS DIAMOND I & II III

A DOPEMAN'S RICHES

HER MAN, MINE'S TOO I, II

By Nicole Goosby

TRAPHOUSE KING **I II & III**

KINGPIN KILLAZ

By **Hood Rich**

LIPSTICK KILLAH **I, II**

CRIME OF PASSION I & II

By **Mimi**

STEADY MOBBN' **I, II**

By **Marcellus Allen**

WHO SHOT YA **I, II**

Renta

GORILLAZ IN THE BAY

DE'KARI

TRIGGADALE

Elijah R. Freeman

GOD BLESS THE TRAPPERS I, II, III

THESE SCANDALOUS STREETS I, II, III

FEAR MY GANGSTA I, II, III

THESE STREETS DON'T LOVE NOBODY I, II

Tranay Adams

THE STREETS ARE CALLING

Duquie Wilson

MARRIED TO A BOSS...

By **Destiny Skai & Chris Green**

BOOKS BY LDP'S CEO, CA$H

TRUST IN NO MAN

TRUST IN NO MAN 2

TRUST IN NO MAN 3

BONDED BY BLOOD

SHORTY GOT A THUG

THUGS CRY

THUGS CRY 2

THUGS CRY 3

TRUST NO BITCH

TRUST NO BITCH 2

TRUST NO BITCH 3

TIL MY CASKET DROPS

RESTRAINING ORDER

RESTRAINING ORDER 2

IN LOVE WITH A CONVICT

Coming Soon

BONDED BY BLOOD 2

BOW DOWN TO MY GANGSTA

Chris Green

www.ingramcontent.com/pod-product-compliance
Lightning Source LLC
Chambersburg PA
CBHW070031260626
47159CB00005B/2018